A Reminder of Stones

A Reminder of Stones

Caine Campbell

Copyright © 2001 by Caine Campbell.

Library of Congress Number:		2001118062
ISBN #:	Hardcover	1-4010-2407-6
	Softcover	1-4010-2408-4

All rights reserved. No part of this book may be reproduced or transmitted in any form or by any means, electronic or mechanical, including photocopying, recording, or by any information storage and retrieval system, without permission in writing from the copyright owner.

This is a work of fiction. Names, characters, places and incidents either are the product of the author's imagination or are used fictitiously, and any resemblance to any actual persons, living or dead, events, or locales is entirely coincidental.

This book was printed in the United States of America.

To order additional copies of this book, contact:
Xlibris Corporation
1-888-7-XLIBRIS
www.Xlibris.com
Orders@Xlibris.com

FOR BETTYE, FOREVER

The Players

CABLE Bannerman. Young sheriff of Joshua County, scion of the pioneering Bannerman family, sole heir to the Bannerman Ranch and the family fortune.

Linda Faye Jernigan. Divorcee close to ten years older than Cable, computer graphics artist at the map company in Gilgal, and Cable's lover.

Benjamin Edes. Editor and publisher of *Harry's of the West*, the daily newspaper in Gilgal.

Dooley Charter. Longtime overseer of the Bannerman Ranch. Helped rear Cable.

Alexander Meredith. Retired architect. Suspect in the Swinton murder.

O. B. World War Two air combat veteran. Musician, plays the upright bass.

Marvin Green. Cable's chief assistant, with rank of detective.

Edward H. "Lucky" Garrison. Proprietor of the Equal Opportunity Car Lot.

Cameron Bannerman. "Ol' Banner," Cable's grandfather, owner of 175,000-acre ranch.
Pepys Fowler. Female deputy sheriff, collects gossip, knows "where the bodies are buried."
Fanny Wright. Young law enforcement intern.
Tom Lenard. Sheriff of Fillmore County in trans-Pecos Texas.
Gideon Lincecum. Defense attorney for Alexander Meredith.

Take twelve men from the people, one from each tribe, and order them to lift up twelve stones from the river. They are to set them down in Gilgal. Thus they will leave a reminder of stones unto the children of Israel forever.

Joshua 4:2-7

Chapter One

JUST inches away from the gas tank of the Trans Am the hard blue flame of an acetylene torch threatened to blow up the car. If it went, with it would go the thief whose hand held the torch, and worse, it would get me. I was standing there with gun drawn. I was there because I had to be. I was sheriff of Joshua County, Texas.

I had walked into the small metal building slowly, and undetected. The thief was occupied with rolling himself on a crawler underneath the Trans Am, trailing the acetylene hoses behind him.

That's when I drew. "The fellow you stole that car from is not hurt bad. So right now all you've got is car theft and minor assault charges against you. But he's fond of that car. I'm fond of him. It better be in sound condition, or I won't take you in on charges. I'll shoot your ass right here."

At my last word, the thief struck the flint, and the torch's blue cut leaped forth. "You're not killing me, and you're not taking me. This whole place is about to blow up."

That's when he jabbed the torch up close to the rear of the gas tank.

What, I thought, had got me in this fix? My whole life did not flash before my eyes, but a pretty good replay of the previous hour did. Since then I've had time to think about it more. I heard one time that each one of us is a story. That little story is part of a bigger story. My bigger story was Joshua County. It was the ranch in Joshua County where I grew up. It was the town of Gilgal. It was the people there and the way they lived. Besides having a sworn duty, I liked most of the folks I was supposed to protect. I, Cable Bannerman, took it as a personal offense when one of 'em got hurt.

Earlier that day I had gotten a call through 911 that there had been a robbery and assault at one of the car lots in Gilgal. Some sorry bastard had beat up "Lucky" Garrison and stolen a car from his show lot.

The owner and sole proprietor of the Equal Opportunity Car Lot had long been lame and years ago had lost his right arm and sight in his left eye. I was enraged by any crime, and particularly by a violent crime, that occurred in my jurisdiction. This one was unacceptable, being committed against a fellow in the shape Lucky was in.

How many times had Edward H. Garrison had to listen to somebody recite the old joke, the classified ad seeking return of a dog. "Blind in one eye, missing an ear, has three legs. Answers to the name 'Lucky'."

"That how you got your nickname? Haw haw haw."

Lucky got to where at the mere mention of a want ad he would cut the interrogator off at the pass.

There was the embarrassing time, and Lucky still regretted it because he was really a kind-hearted fellow, when an ad saleslady from the newspaper called on him. At her saying something about a classified, he so terrified her she ran from the car lot in tears.

Lucky had not had to listen to the abominable anecdote for a long time now. After the incident with the innocent saleslady, he got a little card printed up: "I began with an auto detail shop, before I opened the Equal Opportunity Car Lot. With the waxes and other compounds I used, the finish I achieved became known far and wide as the Garrison finish. My pal Larry 'Lodestone' Weeks, who frequented Bandera Downs and was a lifelong devotee of the sport of kings, told me that the term Garrison finish, long before I ever adopted it, referred to when a winner comes from behind at the last minute. I told him that sure would be lucky. He started calling me Lucky, and it stuck. Do not dare mention that offensive want ad about the dog, or you won't be so lucky."

The thief knocked Lucky in the head, took keys off the board, and raced away in a ten-year-old gunmetal gray Pontiac Trans Am. Of course it bore the now legendary Garrison finish.

When I got to the lot, Lucky was lying on a gurney, refusing EMS transport. A medic had cleaned off the blood and applied a bandage. Lucky was wearing his usual racetrack plaid jacket and contrasting maroon trousers. Chipper as ever, he fixed his one good eye on me. "You'll get the bastard. That I can count on. I'll be all right, but get that Trans Am. It's my favorite on the lot right now."

My chief deputy, Marvin Green, soon drove up.

He had already done all the routine you do when there's a car theft. Marvin also had a lead. "A witness gave me a description that matches up with Warren Bacon. We had a report he was seen over in Kerrville last week, but it was never confirmed. Bacon has a record, not a long record but an ugly record."

Something came to me. There had been a break-in at a cabin a few miles out of town. Nothing was taken, so maybe Bacon had just been looking for a hideout. It was a long shot, but it was the only shot I had.

Soon I was silently making my way to the metal shed out behind the little cabin.

Even with gun drawn, I felt helpless. That in turn made me feel foolish. Seconds ticked away. The thief said no more. I said nothing. The steady rush of the acetylene torch seemed to grow louder. It was that sound, now like a furnace's roar, that got into my mind. Propelled, it seemed, by the force of that sound rather than by my own conscious direction, my left hand went for the Bowie knife in the scabbard at my belt. The tanks, I had finally noticed, were closer to me than they were to the car, close enough for me, without taking a step, just leaning slightly, to slash the hose completely through. The thief's light went out.

Still holding the gun on my captive, I sheathed the knife and closed the valves on the supply tanks. "Roll on out."

When the thief was erect, I put cuffs on him. "Tell me again how you're not going to be taken."

The answer was a look somewhere between sullen and sheepish.

"What's your name?"

Still the thief did not speak.

I gave him a stout push in the chest, knocking him to the concrete floor. Cuffed and unable to break his fall, the thief dropped clumsily. His head struck a gear box, making a nasty cut.

I stood over him. "Your name."

The thief attempted to wipe blood off his cheek and jaw, leaning his head to one side where it would rub against the shoulder of his shirt.

"Bacon."

"Full name."

"Warren Bacon."

I read him his rights. "What were you fixing to do with the torch before I came in?"

"Car has a bad tail pipe. Was going to replace it."

No new pipe was in sight.

I pulled Bacon up from the floor about half way and then just for the hell of it let him drop.

"From what I can see, Lucky's favorite is okay. Lucky for you it is. I'm taking you in. I'll come back for the Trans Am and Lucky'll give it a good going over. You might say your life is in his hands. Or in his hand. He's just got one, you cowardly sonofabitch."

After turning Warren Bacon over to Marvin for booking and leaving Marvin to notify other law enforcement offices where charges were pending, I headed back to the Equal Opportunity Car Lot.

Lucky had said he was okay, and he was. The mild effects of the blow to the head had subsided completely. He had never been willing to give up driving, and had long since mastered a quick maneuver of his one hand and arm from steering wheel to shift lever and back again. He got in the patrol car with me to go fetch the Trans Am.

"Lucky, why do you suppose Bacon chose to steal

that Trans Am? I know it's your favorite, but it's not nearly the price of some of your cars, not as late a model. Besides, that model draws more attention, which Bacon didn't need."

"Maybe he just likes Trans Ams. It's a little old, but it was the only one on the lot."

"Any trouble with the tail pipe?"

"Nosiree."

"He lied about that, just as I thought."

In the patrol car we crossed the four-lane bridge. A couple of miles on the other side of the Guadalupe River I hung a left onto a gravel road.

"Lucky, how'd you come up with a name like Equal Opportunity Car Lot?"

"You wouldn't want me to call it 'Affirmative Action Car Lot,' would you? Where I grew up in East Texas, there were about as many black folks as white folks. When I was just a boy, I began to notice that black fellows always never owned anything but good-looking cars, cars that had style, good design."

"You're talking about used cars."

"Yeah, most of 'em. With the wages they got they couldn't buy new ones. But boy did they have an eye for the sharp car. So I figured you could cut right past what the auto writers said, and just buy what the black fellows were buying. Peckerwoods—that's what we called the white guys over in East Texas—peckerwoods didn't have any damn taste at all when it came to cars."

"There was another used car place where yours is now."

"They had gone broke. Closed the place. I bought it cheap, after checking the Bible."

"The Bible?"

"You need to look for divine guidance, Cable. By

then I had been around Joshua County long enough to know that folks here look first in the Book of Joshua. There it was: 'The second lot came forth!' Joshua 19:1. Actually it read, 'The second lot cast was for Simeon.' So I knew I should open a second car lot on the site of the first one, in spite of the fact that my name wasn't Simeon. But I had a pal named Simeon. Silas O'Riley Simeon. He was the kind of fellow who would like the whole idea of what I was going to do."

Lucky's deciphering of the scripture brought a grin to my face. "I'm beginning to understand how to arrange biblical sanction. First you change the verse to suit yourself."

"If it reads better. That's what the translators who worked for King James did. Don't you know that, Cable?"

"Then if the name mentioned is not yours, but it is the name of a pal, why then you've got your personal message from God! What did you find in the Book of Joshua about Equal Opportunity?"

"Joshua 17:3. 'Zelophehad had no sons but only daughters: their names were Mahlah, Noah, Hoglah, Milcah and Tirzah. They were given a patrimony on the same footing as their father's brothers according to the commandment of the Lord.' But that didn't figure in my plans. I'm just telling you that because you're such a smart-aleck, so damn sarcastic, and so I want you to know there *is* something in the Book of Joshua about Equal Opportunity."

"Well, what did figure in your plans?"

"On the lot right now, I've got cars that black fellows admire, and nothing else. I've got a '64 Mustang. I've got a '65 Buick, one of the small jobs. One of the latest models on the lot is an '88 Chevy

Caprice. There's a Cadillac convertible, the 510 engine. Not long ago I was able to buy a '57 Thunderbird. Got it off a widow. She didn't know what she had. It had belonged to her husband, now deceased, and was stored in the barn."

"You stocked cars like these from the beginning?"

"That was the idea. And I still do. Yesterday I sold a '56 Olds Rocket 88. High compression, four-barrel carburetor. Two-tone, baby blue and powder white. I always have one or more '57 Chevys. Herman Edwards, the master mechanic, told me that car was one mistake General Motors never made again. I asked Mr. Edwards—everybody called him Mr. Edwards—what the mistake was. 'The '57 was so good they couldn't sell the '58s. But they straightened that out. Never made the same mistake again. Never made a car that good again.' You ought to see one I got last week. A '76 Ford Crown Victoria, used to be a police car."

"You haven't mentioned any Chrysler Corporation cars."

"Blacks don't go for 'em much. You notice that? In the '50s the head of Chrysler was asked why his cars were not so good looking. Not realizing his reply was ironic, he said, 'It's not by design.' But black fellows do like, for durability and economy's sake, something with a slant six, like the Dodge Aspen or Plymouth Valiant. You can't beat a slant six."

"Besides this Trans Am we're going for, what's your next favorite in stock right now?"

"Has to be the '76 Davis Continental. Has opera windows and a 460 engine. To translate for you, that's 6.7 liters."

"I never heard of a Davis Continental."

"You should have. Why did the Ford Motor

Company name it after the President of the United States? Why not the President of the Confederacy? Before the war, Jefferson Davis proposed the first continental railway. See the connection? Continental. But they named it a Lincoln Continental. I call it a Davis Continental."

"Of course the Alamobile is a special car. It's not my favorite because it's not what you'd call authentic. It's the one exception to my cars being chosen by the tastes of black fellows. I guess you'd say it's a cowboy's car. Not a real cowboy."

I had seen the Alamobile. "Where'd that thing come from, Lucky?"

"A land speculator who had more money than he knew what to do with wanted to outdo the Texas Cadillacs with longhorns mounted across the hood. He bought a 1949 Rolls Royce, right-hand drive, and got a custom shop to replace the radiator grille, the headlights, the whole front of the car with a replica of the façade of the Alamo. I got the car at a bargain price when the speculator went busted."

"Lucky, there are not many blacks in Joshua County, not enough for you to make a living selling cars to."

"I don't. I sell 'em to whites. That way they get models that are pre-selected, you might say, by the keen eye for style that blacks have demonstrated. It's my way of providing at least a little slice of Equal Opportunity for white folks. And that, Cable, is why I call my place the Equal Opportunity Car Lot."

When we got to the metal shed behind the little cabin, Lucky gave the Trans Am the once-over and declared it to be okay. It cranked right off. He drove it back to the Equal Opportunity Car Lot, and when I joined him he told me it was as good as when it was stolen.

"Lucky, he was going under that car with a cutting torch when I got there. What does that mean to you?"

"To hide contraband in a frame member."

"That's right. Or to take it out. See, that could explain why he took that particular car. Where did you get it?"

"Off an auction in San Antone, about three months ago."

"Well, nothing fishy there, but it could have been a mistake. Somebody let the car go, back down the line, let's say, and Bacon was able to trace it to your place. Will you call the auction and find out what you can?"

"Sure. But why piss around? I'll get my welder to go right in the frame and find the stuff, whatever it is."

We went to the shop, donned helmets, and watched as the welder's flame cut through a likely spot in the frame. Bacon's position on the crawler had provided a clue, and inspection soon revealed a previous weld. After cooling the cut, the welder reached in with gloved hand and drew forth a 2 by 3 1/2 by 5 tin that originally had held two Jack Daniel's miniatures.

"By God, Old No. 7!" exclaimed the welder, and handed the tin to me.

It was heavy, extra heavy for such a small handful. The lid was firmly snapped shut, protecting the cargo the metal box carried, but yielded easily when I pulled it up and open.

All three of us spoke at once, or maybe said nothing, struck speechless, and just thought in unison, "Diamonds!"

Blue diamonds, yellow diamonds, large, medium, and small diamonds, all unmounted diamonds eagerly reflecting and splitting light after a long time shut up in darkness.

Whether our dazzled trio spoke or not, our mouths were wide open, as were our eyes. The welder had never owned a diamond or even given one to his bride and wife. I had several heirloom diamonds, women's jewelry, tucked away and long out of sight at the ranch. Lucky wore a gaudy diamond ring that now seemed to blush instead of sparkle in the overpowering presence of this suddenly released eruption of diamond power.

"Lordy mercy!" cried Lucky.

"How much are they worth?" asked the welder.

"Who do these stones belong to, that's the question," I said.

"Well, it came out of my car," Lucky said with a grin.

"I'll back your claim on it, pal," I replied, "no question there. What I mean is, who did own it, who may try to get it returned. I don't know a damn thing about diamonds, but I'm guessing we may be looking at a million bucks worth."

The welder put the frame member back in order. Then Lucky hiked the price on the Trans Am a couple of hundred and put it back in its prime place on the show lot.

"Get a new card printed up, Lucky," I said.

Lucky looked puzzled.

Gripping the tin of diamonds, I said, "I'll get Marvin to find out who may be missing some diamonds, but often in contraband situations no claim is ever made. Either the diamonds are yours, or you likely get a big reward. Your new card can explain why we call you Lucky."

Chapter Two

I was in the middle of an election campaign. Four years ago, at twenty-four, I had won my first political race to become the youngest sheriff in the history of Joshua County. Now I was trying to win a second term. All the elected county officials in Joshua County were still Democrats, unlike neighboring Kerr County where they had gradually become all Republicans. The people in the two counties weren't different in their views, I liked to tell the Republicans; the folks in Joshua County just had longer memories.

I was a better sheriff than I was a politician. On the plus side, I kept my fences mended in instances like the one with Lucky Garrison. Without being too self-centered about it, I knew that people really liked me for the way I looked after them when they were in need. It came natural to me to enjoy personal contacts. But my friends wanted me to unbend more in public settings.

I tried. One anecdote I added to my campaign

speeches had to do with the decline in the fortunes of Democrats in Kerr County. I would bring up the Elvis Presley sightings and other sightings like that, and then inquire of the audience, "Have you gotten word of any Albert Packer sightings over in Kerr County? You recall Packer, don't you? He was one of a half-dozen gold prospectors who went into the mountains in the dead of winter. There, they were overcome by the worst snows ever and by starvation. Only Packer survived. The other five were hacked to death and their flesh devoured by surviving companions, until only Packer remained. At the end of the villain's trial, the judge announced the sentence:

"Packer, you Republican, man-eating son of a bitch, there were five Democrats in Hinsdale County, an' you voracious bastard hev eaten 'em all! I sentence you to be hanged by the neck until you're daid, as a solemn warnin' agin' redoocin' the Democratic population of this county."

I had already won the Democratic nomination, against one weak opponent. Sometimes the word "tantamount," which I had heard often as a boy, would start going around and around in my head. Damn, I wished it was still true. But I had an uncommonly formidable Republican opponent in the general election which was now just a month away. And I had made some enemies. Mostly I was glad of that.

I told this Packer anecdote only at rallies attended by males or mostly males. Word spread that I was using some coarse language in public, but it didn't seem to hurt. People in their sixties and seventies thought of me as old Banner's grandson, or that Bannerman boy, so they shook their heads and said "Boys will be boys."

I did nothing to lower the level of political humor, maybe raised it a little. That's not saying much. My Republican opponent was an admirer of Bob Dole's acerbic wit. He liked to repeat Dole's quip about the reunion of three ex-presidents: "Carter, Ford, and Nixon—See No Evil, Hear No Evil, and Evil."

Only in post-election conversation would any conclusions be drawn about what lost the Republican the election. Maybe his Dole-style wisecracks cost him votes. What did seem evident was that he foundered in the last couple of weeks of the campaign. I won big.

I had been elected to the first term on the basis of my general appeal and my reputation. One voter, a woman, told me after my first race that she voted for me because, at six-two, I was the tallest candidate for sheriff. Another woman told me that I got her vote because I looked like a movie star. Well, those were not her exact words. She said, "I voted for you" and then she asked, "Anybody ever tell you that you look like Brad Pitt?"

Then it burned in my gut for the people to re-elect me because I had been a good sheriff for four years. They had done it, by a sixty-forty margin, so I could relax. I felt free to indulge myself in some "intellectual matters." In my mind I resisted the description, but that's what it amounted to.

Benjamin Edes was going to help me. With the election over, I would have more time to spend with Ben.

Several years earlier I had become the sole heir of our vast family ranch, reckoned in square miles instead of acres, handed down in the family since the grant from Spain in the early 1800s. The cattle business wasn't what it used to be, but outside investments paid handsomely, and there was income from steep fees charged to hunters. I didn't need to be sheriff for the pay. After Army service and combat in the bloody action in Graustark, law enforcement was something I wanted to do or maybe had to do.

I just enjoyed the hell out of being hard on criminals. I stayed within the law. There had been times when I wanted to shoot culprits on the spot. My ancestors had had to kill to get land and had to kill to keep it. I believed in the tradition of frontier justice and was proud of it.

"You're only justifying this barbaric trait of yours," Ben Edes would tell me. "But if you're going to justify it, do it right. Learn more about your forebears, more about ranching history. Learn why they killed, how they killed. Read more literature so you gain a better understanding of human motivation."

Ben's remarks had become a challenge to me. I was proud of my forebears, and I wanted to keep the tradition going. Now, however, I didn't have to make sense of my inclinations to myself alone. I also had to make sense of it for Ben.

I led my force easily. The operation ran smoothly. Early in my first term I had made a key appointment. In the detective slot I had placed Marvin Green. Noted for his forensic skills and compulsive record-keeping, Marvin was about zero in imagination. I could rely on Marvin for all the tedium of crime scene discipline and investigative legwork. I could be the genius detective. That's what I liked. I didn't enjoy the boring, routine part of crime work or any of the administrative chores that came with being sheriff.

A smile was more likely to come to my face when

I was alone than when I was in company. I smiled now, on this first morning after re-election, content and assured with a full term behind me, and, ahead of me, more time for sparring with Ben Edes.

The telephone rang. The smile vanished.

"Yeah."

Marvin Green was on the line. "I'm in the car out on 50. Dispatcher called in a killing. I think."

"What do you mean, you think?"

"I've already had a look. There's a body. This one's different, Cable. It's Phil Swinton, dead in his home. In the bathroom."

It was damn sure different, I thought. In the first term all the homicides had been in convenience store hold-ups, domestic fights, that kind of thing. Nobodies. Phil Swinton owned a bank, had served one term as mayor of Gilgal, county seat of Joshua County. "You're not sure it was a killing?"

"Cause of death was a gunshot. But . . . listen, Cable, meet me there, or I'll pick you up. It's hard to describe on the phone."

"Pick me up. I'll go on out the back steps." I hung up.

What happened to my leisurely second term? I thought.

Phil G. Swinton was not a man whose company you sought, unless you had to have a loan from his bank. With close-set eyes and thin lips, he was one of those pinch-faced, inward, ill-natured bastards you would avoid if you could. But you had to admit that he thought clearly, like the time he put in a new lavatory. Experiencing a bout of lower back pain, he found that even a simple act like shaving was excruciating. Bending over a low lavatory to wash his face and rinse his razor was the problem. Why, he wondered, were lavatories installed so low? Even if you didn't have back pain they were an inconvenience to a full-grown man. Their height must have been determined by compromise, when a house would have only one lavatory, so the children could reach it. Hell, he didn't have any children, and he had several lavatories. At least one of them could be at a proper height for shaving.

The thought crystallized when he had shaved only the left side of his face. Without even rinsing off the remaining lather, he headed for the telephone, called Nathan Osborne, the plumber, offered him a bonus for an emergency service call, then waited.

In less than an hour, Nathan had installed a small lavatory exactly four and a half feet from the floor. Then Swinton re-lathered the right side of his face and with immense satisfaction resumed shaving, standing erect and not having to stoop to rinse.

Directly across from the little sink was where I now saw the body. Swinton could have looked up and seen his prized lavatory from there if he hadn't been dead.

Marvin, his coal-black hair slicked back, was in charge of the scene just as I expected him to be. His boots, with the style of heels he liked, made him appear taller than the five-ten he was.

Marvin stood next to me, describing what had been too complicated to convey over the telephone. "See the entry wound, just about in the abdomen? Medium caliber is my guess, fired dead on. Unless the body was shoved around afterwards, he would have had to have been standing at his little special lavatory. He could hold a weapon, using both hands, and do it himself, but there's no weapon in sight. Seems to rule out suicide, but listen to the best part:

Swinton protected the whole house with a standard grade security system, but his living quarters—this bathroom, a bedroom, and a sitting room—are like a vault. Just one door for entry and it's a stout one, plus the best locks and a super high quality detection and alarm system for this suite. It is one hell of a casemate. And it was all locked tight from the inside when the body was discovered!"

I backed out of the bathroom, repelled by the impossibly knotty case confronting me: a corpse, but no weapon, and no visible means of entry to the murder scene.

From outside the bathroom door, I spotted a small card taped to the lavatory, missed when I had crowded into the room and virtually had my back to the sink.

"What's it say, Marvin?"

The card bore neat lettering. The deputy had read it earlier, but to make no mistake peered closely to read it aloud.

"Greetings from Gropius."

Chapter Three

THE Gropius calling card diverted Marvin and me, for a time, away from the implausibility of what appeared to have happened to the late Phil G. Swinton. We went to work on what meaning the card offered.

Marvin straightened his badge and reached for the Gilgal phone book. "Nobody would use his own name, I guess, but it's a place to start. Here's Groff. Grogan. Groll. Grona. Gropper. No Gropius."

"Try the Hill Country book," I offered. Additional exchanges were listed there.

"Okay, let's see. It has the same ones . . . more of some of 'em. After Grona there's Gropeen. Still no Gropius."

"This is a trail so cold it'll get no colder." I was set to work out my own quandary, and even a murder was not going to stop me. "Do all the usual stuff, and let me know when you get the pathology. I've got somebody to go see."

I made a perfunctory rap on the door jamb and walked into the open office of Benjamin Edes, editor and publisher of Gilgal's daily newspaper, *Harry's of the West*.

"Howdy, Ben," I said.

Ben had already looked up from his Royal typewriter where on the old manual he was finishing today's editorial. "Your timing's great, Cable. I need to get something on the Swinton killing."

I recited the particulars, ending on the Gropius note. "Go ahead and put that in your story. It might have some effect on the killer. Killers do read your newspaper, don't they Ben? How do you feel about a killer reading your editorials, the comics, the classifieds?"

"In this business you just have to resolve yourself to the fact that a newspaper is a public facility. Anybody can use it."

"You mean like a toilet over in the courthouse."

"Ah, the sheriff shows a touch of humor today. I don't believe the sheriff is totally consumed by his new murder case."

"I wish I were. As usual, I'm preoccupied with what we've talked about before."

"Go after it. Okay. Chase it down. Keep three things on your mind: learning, and learning, and learning. If that's not exciting enough for your hell-faring character, then make it discovery, discovery, discovery."

"Where do I start? Or where do I re-start? You've been educating me for several years."

"You had already been 'educated' when we met, Cable. Had a degree from Texas A & M, had some Army schools. Trouble is you had never really been introduced to the higher learning. It can be said of only a few colleges that after you graduate, the Army is a liberalizing experience. But it can be said of A & M."

Ben was a graduate of T.C.U. In my view that was better than being a Tea Sipper, a University of Texas ex, but not much better. He enjoyed making barbs at the expense of my alma mater.

"The place to re-start is where you left off," Ben continued. "This time, however, you start specializing. I want you to read more Texas history, but get to the ranching history, the really revealing stuff that shows you what your family forebears were likely doing, were enduring, fifty and a hundred years ago."

"Looking for skeletons?"

"Not really. You're looking for flesh-and-blood fellows who lived in rough times. They prospered in those times, so that means they met roughness with roughness. Paraphrasing Ward Allen, their fight was often shield to shield."

Ben kept in his office some relics of the old days of newspapering. He had a "hellbox" for discarded type in spite of the fact there had been no lead type in his plant for thirty years. One piece, called an "imposing stone," was a large slab, mounted countertop high, not needed since the days of hot type production for letterpress. He got up from the chair at his desk, walked over to the imposing stone and leaned on it on his elbow, looking out the window.

"My family doesn't figure in any of these books you're talking about," I said.

"Good minds run in your family, but, like yours, they don't run to reflection. As you've told me, none of them ever wrote down anything about themselves except births, deaths, and marriages in the family Bible. So the best you can do is get the sense, the setting. That's what you'll get from the books. To put it in the vernacular, you've seen one ranch family, you've seen them all."

"You know what I'm after, Ben. I enjoy the human chase. I would enjoy killing a criminal, if I had the law's sanction."

"You could see a shrink, of course. But what would that do for the reputation of our classic Texas lawman, the high sheriff of Joshua County? Besides, you know my conviction that contemplation of the past—anybody's past—is good therapy, with effects similar to dredging up your own personal past on the couch."

It was my turn for sarcasm. "You're expecting a lot from an Aggie background."

"No, I expect very little, especially after you described Marvin and you thumbing through the telephone book looking for Gropius! If you had benefited from a good liberal arts education, you would have gone to a biographical dictionary instead of a telephone directory."

"To find his address and phone number?"

"Not likely. Gropius died in the '60s. But you could have learned his first name. Walter. He was founder of the Bauhaus school of architecture, of what came to be called modernism. It had its counterparts in literature and the fine arts, and of course there were inner contradictions, but simply put, modernism, especially in architecture, held the view that if you put people in better living structures, they'll be transformed into better people."

"So do I look for a suspect who grew up in a public housing project?"

"I don't know what you look for. That doesn't necessarily give you a connection to the late Mayor

Swinton, in any case. But it does give you a tidbit that might match up with something else you come across. I'll admit it's not as direct as if you and Marvin could get his number, call him, and ask him to come turn himself in!"

I know my poise must have drooped a little bit as Ben chuckled. I said, "Go ahead, rub it in."

Ben's chuckle segued into a soft smile. "If I were rubbing it in, I'd suggest you and Marvin go look in the San Antonio white pages. Lots more pages. Lots more names. Lots more chance you'd find Gropius!"

I liked a lot of things about Linda Faye. I couldn't think of anything I didn't like about her. I thought of her now.

I rang her number at home. In that throaty alto which in itself delivered a message that warmed me all over, Linda Faye's "hello there" came over the line.

"Linda Faye, this is Cable. You're on my mind, darlin'."

A tantalizing combination of "Oh-h-h" and "aw-w-w," and then "Ca-a-a-ble," like it took all day to say my name.

I said nothing for a moment and let the sensation pulse through me. I felt a tightening in my pants, thinking *this is adolescent* to feel this way just hearing Linda Faye over the telephone.

"Linda Faye, let's get together." We were already together, in a way that transcended marriage vows, common sense, and telephone lines. Linda Faye had been married just the once, had no children, and had been divorced about two years now. At 38, she was close to ten years older than I. We had been seeing each other about a year.

"Whatcha got in mind?" she asked.

"I'll never tell."

"Oh-h-h-aw-h-h, Cable, don't do this to me," Linda Faye teased.

"They've got a little band down at the American Legion in Bandera tonight, Brier Patch. They're good. Play some deep south country blues and a little western swing."

"That's swang, Cable, swang." Then, again like it took her all day to say it, "When are you com-m-ming for me?"

I gulped. Would we be able to get out of her place, once I was there, and on to the dance? "I'll be there in a jiffy."

Linda Faye knew what that meant. I would go by my apartment, change out of my uniform, and show up at her place in less than an hour.

"Hurry, Cable, you got to hurry, honey."

Later, at her door, a warm embrace threatened the dance card, but somehow we managed to become two again, get in my car, and head for Bandera.

It was my own car we traveled in, a habit of mine meant to gain as much privacy as possible when off duty. To distinguish it from my county patrol vehicle, Linda Faye called it the "cable car." I thought that was cute. Worldly-wise as I thought of myself as being, I became a boy in her care and thought everything she said or did was cute.

Brier Patch lived up to advance billing, and Linda Faye enjoyed it. The only sour note for her was when, at my urging, the band did their cover of Johnny Paycheck's "Pardon Me, I've Got Somebody to Kill." For Linda Faye, it was too close to the truth about the trait in me that troubled her. I treated the song as something amusing. Linda Faye didn't think it was funny.

The crowd was sparse, and only a few folks spoke with me, congratulating me on my election victory. Truth is, no matter how much attention I got, I counted a night in a dance spot a success if no fight broke out. I thought about tales O. B. had told me, of playing in a band in honky tonks where they had to put up chicken wire around the bandstand to keep boisterous patrons from roughing up band members. "But when I played," O. B. boasted, "they had to cage us in with chicken wire to keep me from attacking the dancers!"

Fights didn't break out in American Legion halls anyway. That was only one of the reasons I liked to come here. The bar was just like being back in an Army club. Fellows rolled dice out of the leather dice cups, playing "Horses" for drinks. Occasionally some eager new follower would be ceremoniously inducted into the Order of Turtles. The origin of the practice is lost in the fog of many smoky Army and Navy bars over many years of camaraderie. In all the U.S. uniformed services, a new soldier or sailor is asked if he wants to belong to the Order. Upon his assent, he is told that whenever he may be asked, "Are you a Turtle?," no matter the place, no matter who may be within hearing, he must reply, "You bet your sweet ass I am." It is a solemn vow, made in the presence of comrades in arms. Given the experience of the Legionnaire membership, most of them already Turtles, there were few inductions.

As we were leaving, Brier Patch broke into their Tex-Mex version of "Tuxedo Junction." They called it "Tostito Junction."

Back at Linda Faye's place, and lying close to her,

everything washed away. There had been no election, there would never be another election, there had been no murder, I wouldn't need to talk with Ben again, I was not obsessed with thoughts about my own character, I would read no more Texas books.

Chapter Four

AT a table in the Gilgal town library the next morning, I hunched over *Tales of Old-Time Texas*. It was no history, but it was on Ben's list. J. Frank Dobie's retelling of folk tales was a painless way for me to ease into the chore I had set for myself.

I liked to read here. I had kept a small apartment in town since becoming sheriff, a handy and comfortable place, but not inspiring. The ranch house was etched with inspiration. It was also a forty-mile drive, out in the western part of the county. The two-story library building provided atmosphere enough. Built and furnished in the 1920s, its masculine and somewhat dark, oaken character just seemed to invite you to read and reflect. Nobody looking for law enforcement would find me in the library unless they happened upon me. I didn't let the dispatcher know when I came here. Only Marvin knew.

I looked up from the Dobie. There was Marvin.

"I was waiting for you to get to a stopping place."

"Well, Marvin, I have stopped now. What's up?"

"All the forensics are in. No surprises, and we didn't have any reason to expect any. The slug came from a 9 millimeter, probably an import, thirty or forty years old. Hard to trace an old foreigner like that. Not that we have much to trace, with no weapon in hand."

Our conversation had attracted attention. "Let's go over to the courthouse and have a look," I whispered, closing the Dobie without inserting a bookmark.

I had an office that was roomy but not huge. My only real luxury to befit my position was a twenty-by-forty space, accessible only through my office. There evidence and other investigative materials could be spread out on four big tables, tacked on walls, set up on easels, and examined piece by piece or viewed in the large. I called the room "case prep." Marvin and I worked there when trying to solve a crime. Then I let the prosecutors use it to prepare a case to go to court and nail the defendant.

I followed Marvin from display to display, saying nothing until the deputy had concluded his exposition.

"There's nothing here, Marvin. Everything is here, and nothing is here. But we're going to track us a suspect. Not the killer. There's no trail. We are going to track the deceased. We are going to get on the trail of the late Phil G. Swinton. He did something to somebody to get himself killed. Maybe more than one somebody, maybe last week, maybe twenty years ago."

"At least we know the name of the quarry."

"That's right, Marvin. And we know his address and telephone number." The joke was lost on Marvin.

I continued. "We've got gossip, and we've got the newspapers. If there's any difference." I'd have to remember to repeat this gibe to one Benjamin Edes.

"I'll send Pepys to do the gossip," Marvin said. "She can gossip with the best of them." Pepys Fowler, pronounced 'Peeps,' was a woman deputy.

"Get our new intern, what's her name . . ."

"Fanny Wright."

"Yeah, get Fanny to go through the bound volumes of back issues over at the paper office. Fanny was a research assistant at Sam Houston State, probably be good at it. Ben will help her get started. Tell her to look up the years when Swinton was mayor. That would be the time when he had the greatest scope for infuriating people, although the mean sonofabitch, pardon me, the deceased, didn't need much scope."

Harry's of the West didn't have what newspaper people call a "morgue," where clips from papers are systematically filed and cross-indexed. You couldn't go in a file marked "Swinton" and find all the clips. You had to go through the bound back issues, one by one. The paper generally ran eight pages, sixteen or twenty on Wednesdays, and came out five days a week. There was no paper on Saturday and Sunday. The task would be manageable, even if daunting.

Marvin was on his way out of case prep. "I'll get 'em going," he said over his shoulder.

I called it field day. The deputies called it hell. There had not been one since several weeks before the election. It was time for one today, my memorandum on the bulletin board announced. The deputies were lined up abreast when I walked into the exercise yard. They snapped to attention as they always did here but never did anywhere else. I put them at ease.

"Each of you take a place behind one of those fifty-gallon drums. Think of it as a barrier, your barrier. Be ready to defend yourself against an attacker. I'll be the attacker." They still didn't know what was coming.

From a large, innocuous-looking carton, I took two bulging plastic bags that looked to hold about two quarts each. More were inside the carton. These I had prepared myself with no help from Marvin. On field day, even Marvin could not be trusted with a secret.

I advanced to the first "station," one of the drums protecting a crouching deputy. As the deputy rose slightly to defend his position, brandishing a baton, I brought down the jiggling bag which split open when it hit the baton and delivered its contents on the deputy. I had mixed red dye in milk. The simulated blood oozed down the deputy's face, dripped off his nose and chin, and made a splattered mess of most of his uniform. In almost the same motion I had delivered a bloody assault on a second deputy nearby. Now the others were forewarned, but it did no good except to save them shock and surprise, because the baton, their best defensive weapon, was no shield against my crimson circumstance. The stick even served to help the bag burst.

Foul expletives were shortly followed by laughter all around. My combat exercise today had been messy but brief. I myself was mighty pleased. I liked to see a lot of blood, even if it was on my loyal defenders.

It was dusk when I went to my apartment. With traces of light left in the sky, I made a round of the very small backyard. I headed for Lady. She was the rambling kind, a yellow rose adorned with small blossoms that grew in clusters. Often she was called a ranch rose, a hardy native that grew casually out in the country. Some few called her by her full name, Lady Banksia. Lady's sister bushes were all over the Bannerman Ranch, and last week I had planted just this one to give my utilitarian lodging its only homey touch. I peered at the lattice to see if Lady had begun to attach her tendrils for support.

Something was amiss. Barely visible in the dusk, it was only a hint of intrusion. I took my flash from my belt. With its sharp light, I could make out the smooth prints of somebody's shoes in the roughness of the bed I had made for Lady. Closer scrutiny revealed a cigarette butt. It was plain the intruder had lingered.

"Keep your eyes open, Lady," I muttered. "Somebody's after us."

Chapter Five

KNOWING that I was being stalked ought not to have brought alarm to me, because I'm the sheriff. I can handle it. Looked at another way, I had more reason for concern than an ordinary citizen, because a stalker who would be daring enough to target the sheriff has got to be dangerous. Desperate, maybe, and therefore extra dangerous.

I thought about it this way, decided to treat it seriously, and decided to tell Marvin about it.

"Maybe Swinton's killer thinks you know more than you do, thinks you're on to him."

"If he realized that we know nothing, maybe he would stay the hell out of my flower bed."

"Maybe he's confident you're still in the dark. Maybe you're number two on the murder list after Swinton."

"Maybe it's got nothing to do with Swinton."

"Fanny is plowing away in the old newspapers. Swinton was mayor just for one term, but that's still four years of papers. I don't expect to hear anything from her today."

I headed for the door. "In that case, I'm going to the ranch. Don't look for me until the end of the day."

The regimen set for me by Ben was proving too slow and roundabout to suit me. My understanding had deepened some as I soaked up Texas lore, but I craved something more direct, more personal. I was going to the ranch to sit around awhile with Dooley Charter.

The old fellow had been on the Bannerman spread since before I was born, working for my late grandfather, Cameron Bannerman, and now for me. What he was, was hard to say. Dooley had never had much to do with the cattle or with the hands. He looked after things around the ranch house, but it was off the mark to call him a housekeeper. He tended the wells and the windmills and the other equipment and machinery on the place, but you couldn't call him a mechanic, either. Mostly he saw that repairs got done instead of fixing things himself.

At the ranch, I found Dooley leaning against a fence post at the edge of the ranch house yard. It was Dooley's favorite place, his favorite stance. Keeping his gaze on a far pasture, he didn't turn to look at me until I spoke.

"Anybody stole any grass, Dooley?"

"Keep an eye on it, nobody will."

"I've come out so you can keep an eye out for me for a spell. So I won't get lost. Being away from the ranch so much, I get to feeling adrift."

Beckoning to a bench shaded by the infinity of a live oak tree, Dooley led me over to take a seat there with him.

I asked Dooley, "When you keep count of the blades of grass, you ever spot any bankrupt weed?" We called it 'bankrupt weed' because its appearance on somebody's place was an indication of overgrazing. It was mealycup sage.

Dooley knew I was needling him. "Cable, don't start that stuff with me. You know we're in good shape here. Always have been."

Indeed we had. I was running about 1,200 head on the ranch, all of them longhorns. Not all of the 175,000 acres was grazing land, but there was enough that the cattle got no supplemental feed. Longhorns require little care, foraging and looking out for themselves pretty much as if they were deer in the wild. We only worked about a dozen hands on the place, half of them Mexican-Americans, all legal. Usually we had twenty-five or so horses, probably more than we needed.

"Dooley, I'm looking for something. Somewhere in a nook or cranny of this place, are there any letters, photographs, scrapbooks that any of the family left?"

"There's lots of nooks and crannies. No paper. 'Cept the ranch books. Nothin' but numbers. Dollar numbers, cow numbers. And lately, I been countin' the blades of grass. Puttin' that in the ranch books."

A wry grin announced Dooley's acknowledgment of my gibe.

"But you know all that. You've looked before."

It was the reply I expected; the question about letters and scrapbooks was just my way of easing into the line of inquiry I meant to put to Dooley. Because of the paucity of written records of the family, as a boy I had been fascinated by the big tome, close to four inches thick, with a multi-colored title page proclaiming it to be the "Illustrated Family Bible."

At midpoint were the lined pages bearing elaborately lettered headings for Marriages, Births, and Deaths. The date of publication was 1882, but the first entry, a Cable marriage, was from 1879, as if there had been catching up to do after the acquisition of the mighty Bible. The most recent entries I saw, at that time, were the dates of the deaths of my mother and father and the date of my own birth. Later it had fallen to me to make an entry upon the death of my grandfather, and I adopted the style I saw there on the pages, used first in 1882: Cameron Bannerman. Departed this life on the 21st July, 1979.

Only two pieces of correspondence had been tucked into the book. One was typewritten, dated November 15, 1922. It was a sympathy note, on the occasion of a death in our family, from Dr. & Mrs. Westbrook in Sipe Springs.

My favorite, that I read over and over when I was eleven or twelve, was handwritten in ink on lined paper and headed Angelina, Texas, July 5, 1901: Dear little Willie. Guess you think I'm not going to answer your letter but I'll just suprise you once. I was waiting untill after the 4 to write. You ought to of been with us you would of had such a nice time. I certainly did have a fine *old* time. I only had three *escorts*, but My My! My best fellow he rode up here to spend the fourth. What kind of time did you have? Guess you had a fine time did you not? Say what has become of Mr Milling. You have not spoke of him lately. I have a new fellow Mr Leech Causey. I think he is real good looking. They was two weddings in this part of the world on the third. Willis Brigman to Mollie Jones. Ed Nobles to Donnie Lewis. I guess they will be several weddings over here between now and Christmas. I have not wrote you in some time but still I have no news of enterest to write. They was an old man died last Monday was a week ago. He died from the hiccups he had them nine days. He was a good man. It was a Mr Tillery they say he was an enfidel. I have met him several times but know nothing about him. Well I have wrote all the news I can call to memory at the present. Will close with love and best wishes to all, Write soon to your true . . . Cousin Minnie. Address you letters to Angelina Texas.

I continued my questioning of Dooley. "You may think this is pointless curiosity, but I enjoy making a criminal suffer when I've got him tracked down. I've become convinced—I guess I should say Ben Edes has convinced me—that I should know more about my bloodline."

I noticed a quick tic of defensiveness in Dooley's usually impassive face. What had I hit on?

"Maybe you can remember things, Dooley. Maybe you can tell me something that will help."

Dooley sat a long time, saying nothing.

I waited.

"Next time you're out here, I'll show you something." Dooley had made his decision. He wouldn't act on the spur of the moment. He had to let it settle in. But I knew he wouldn't change his mind.

"Show me . . . what? You said there weren't any papers."

"No paper. Something you'll see."

Dooley lapsed back into silence.

Rising at last, he said, "There's one thing to look at today."

I followed him into the great hall where the Springfields were. I had long walked past the muskets and rifles, each in its own separate place, mounted on a single rack, the collection stretching out one by one along the wall. I had walked without really noticing, as one will trod unseeing a hallway where reposes a family gallery of photographs. This time I noticed. I began with an inspection of the Model 1842 musket, a .69 caliber. Next to it hung a Model 1842 artillery musketoon.

Dooley pointed to the 1855 rifle-musket, reminding me that it, like most of the Springfields there, had been acquired contemporaneously with their issue. They had been acquired to be used, and had been used, by generations of Bannermans. Next to the 1855 was another rifle-musket, the Model 1858 Cadet.

"Those fellows weren't collectors, they were shooters," Dooley remarked. "It was your granddaddy who finally looked on it as a collection and put 'em in here on this wall. He regularly used many of 'em and cleaned all of 'em. Since he died, I've done that—the cleaning, that is. More cleaning than shooting.

"He was the first one, too, to buy just for the sake of owning one. He never could find a Morse, the first breechloader to take a metallic cartridge that was ever made at the Springfield Armory. Only sixty were completed; that was in 1859. Bob Penny has one, but Ol' Banner had to do without. He did find and buy that 1861 musket there, and the one next to it, the 1863. He didn't really want two so much alike, but the fellow he bought 'em off of made him a price for the pair."

We moved on to the 1870 .50/70 rifle. I recalled being told that the Circassian walnut stock had been crafted for my great-grandfather, replacing the original Springfield stock.

"I can remember seeing old Banner fire this 1873 'trapdoor' rifle," I said.

"They got a lot of use out of that one," Dooley replied. "Now this next one, the Model 1903, with the French walnut stock, this was a workhorse. So was the other 1903, with a California 'Claro' stock. As you know, there are two or three more 1903s that don't hang here because they're so often used."

I looked at the Hornet .22, the 'varmint' rifle. "This is one I've used a lot."

I stopped at the next to last rack. It was empty. Until this point nothing had seemed out of the ordinary. I told Dooley, "There's room for another Springfield. I never had noticed."

"That's what I wanted you to see. You see things all your life, so they look right to you. Another 1903 was there. Hung there for years. Why it was took down, that's what I'm going to tell you."

I barely glanced at the last weapon displayed, an M-1 Garand gas-operated semi-automatic. There was no M-14.

I could only accept Dooley's slow pace of disclosure. I asked no more, and walked out of the hall.

As I drove under the great limestone arch, leaving the ranch, a glint of sun off metal or glass caught my eye, down a rut of a road to my left, off the ranch property. I braked, made a sharp turn, and headed for whatever it was that looked out of place amidst juniper, grass, and scrubby oaks.

The rut, which looked to go nowhere, in fact was a shortcut to the paved road. I was too late. By the time I came in sight of the road, the vehicle—that must be what it was—had turned onto the pavement. Whether towards Gilgal or deeper into the country,

I couldn't tell. I was left with a swirl of dust kicked up where the rut met the road and a crawly feeling that I was indeed somebody's quarry.

Linda Faye and I had made a date for that night at her place. After a light supper that Linda Faye had fixed, and a drink or two, we cuddled on the couch, my head in her lap.

"You haven't told me much about what you and Ben talk about, and it's none of my business . . ."

"Darlin,' everything I do, everything I say, is your business. At least I'd like for you to think of it that way."

"You're an unusual fellow, Cable Bannerman, not to want to shut me out of some parts of your life, the 'guy' parts that most men don't figure a woman has any say in. Well, I'm not asking what you talk about with Ben, and I'm not jealous of the time you spend with him. You've got to believe me on that. And I wouldn't dare ask you not to get help from him on your search for answers. I just want to tell you—this is what I'm working up to, Cable—let me comfort you. Whatever you may get from your talks with Ben can't match the warmth of a woman."

I snuggled a little bit. It was my way of agreeing.

"Cable, tell me something. When was the last time you killed somebody in the line of duty?"

I looked away. I said nothing.

"Cable, how many people have you killed as sheriff, all put together?"

"Look, it's not the actual killing, it's the urge to kill."

"You haven't killed one solitary soul, have you." It was not a question. "Since you left the Army."

"In fact I haven't, Linda. But like I said, it's the urge that bothers me."

"That's what I'm getting at. You're a good fellow. You haven't killed anybody. You're upset with yourself because you think you'd like to. That's your conscience. You've got a conscience. I'm glad you have, but you're over-dramatizing this whole thing . . . I think." And Linda smiled.

"You know I wouldn't take this kind of sharp talk from anybody else. Not even from some other woman." Linda's smile turned into a smug smile.

"That big ranch you grew up on was supposed to have been a place full of family. But the way you've made it sound, it was like it was depopulated by the time you came along. Your granddaddy didn't have any brothers or sisters, his wife, your grandmama, died fairly young, they only had one son, your daddy, and no girls, and then you've told me your own mama and daddy went off and left you."

"I feel like they did. They were going to come back for me, if they hadn't been killed in that car crash. I think they were coming back. It has always given me kind of a feeling that maybe they did just go off and leave me."

"Whatever they did, Cable, the result was that there weren't any women around to love you. My goodness, that alone would make a man into a damn mean killer!"

Linda Faye's tone had turned humorous toward the last. I was conscious of it, just as I was conscious of almost everything. Her combination of serious talk and light, almost teasing expression was wonderful, just like everything about her. God! how I loved Linda Faye!

Chapter Six

Linda Faye Jernigan was the daughter and only child of Jackson Jernigan and his wife Belle who lived in Galveston. Linda Faye was born there, grew up there. Respectable, white collar, with a comfortable but modest income, Jackson and Belle paid Linda Faye's way through Texas Tech.

She majored in English and minored in art, making her one of the few visual artists who could write—or think.

After she was graduated from Tech, Linda Faye took a job with a map company in Gilgal, doing computer text and graphics. That's where she met Felix Post. Felix was the press foreman at the map company.

Felix was not like any other man Linda Faye had ever taken an interest in. He was about her own height, 5' 6," while she had always liked 6 footers or better. Only a few years older than she, he was already pattern bald. The ink-black hair he had left he kept trimmed fairly short. He slicked it down with Brilliantine until Linda Faye finally persuaded him to stop. "Lyndon Johnson used it," he would say. "If it was good enough for LBJ, it ought to be good enough for me."

"Lyndon stopped using it when something really important happened to him, when Kennedy was assassinated and Lyndon became President of the United States of America. Something really important has happened to you. You've met me."

Felix was far from gregarious and kept to himself, but oddly he was outspoken when one-to-one, especially with a woman. In fact he had an intensity about him that approached magnetism. *This must be it*, Linda Faye thought one day when she was dressing to go to work. *This must be why I spend time with this weirdo.* There! She had thought it. She had tried not to, but now she had. Alone in her apartment, she decided to speak the word out loud. "Weirdo." Then she tried never to think it again.

There were not all that many eligibles around Gilgal, so Linda Faye, as attractive as she was and as popular with men as she had long been, found herself agreeing to marry eccentric Felix.

His intensity, his bluntness, which had had its charm, turned into incessant verbal bullying. It took Linda Faye close to a year to know she had had enough. She divorced Felix. His personality gave the potential for him to become a stalker, Linda Faye worried. But Felix surprised her. Another facet of his personality kicked in. He was a loner. He quit his job at the map company, pulled up stakes, and cut himself off from her completely. She didn't even know where he went, just parts unknown. Of that she was glad. She had asked no alimony, just the nearly inconsequential equity in the small place they had bought, so happily, just before their wedding. When she was done with Felix, she was really done.

Linda Faye stayed at her job and thus was still in Gilgal when I returned from the Army. From the first time I saw her, I was smitten. I loved her brownish "tweed" eyes and her light brown hair. She was a regular at the beauty shop, but you couldn't tell she had a hair-do. She just looked natural, casually neat, just right.

Linda Faye loved to cook. I would have been a suitor, everything else aside, I often thought, just to hang around and eat her breads, cakes, pies, and cookies. She loved to ride a horse, too, making me think, *Is this woman perfect, or what?*

Linda Faye jumped at any chance to go riding, on the big mare that she favored and that I had virtually given her, but I had to coax her to get her to play the piano and sing. I did coax her and she did play and sing. Her natural style and her seductive alto voice were treasures, private treasures for me as it turned out since she was so shy about it.

Her favorite perfume of course immediately became my favorite perfume—*Knowing*. All her outfits were simple, I noticed at the start, and everything she wore looked right on her. She fancied caps, and cute little hats in fall and winter. In evenings she wore gloves and long socks. They were the last things she took off.

My notice on the bulletin board announced that it was field day again. The deputies trudged to the exercise compound complaining. It was too soon after the recent blood bath. Once there, hopes began to rise when scuttlebutt spread that Marvin had been sent for a load of watermelons. They had been instructed to come with their scabbards strapped on. Each one held a contemporary version of the Bowie knife, like the one I wore. In their minds, we were going to enjoy a watermelon cutting. They would need the knives, they reasoned, to slice the watermelons.

Soon an old stake-body truck full of watermelons rolled into the compound. As Marvin explained to me, he had found a fellow at one of those roadside locations and made a deal with him. He would bring the whole load, so there'd be plenty, and then I would pay him for what was used.

I had kept the deputies at attention longer than usual; I did not put them at ease now. "It's every man for himself. On my command, head for that truck. Unsheathe your knife, and attack those damn watermelons. Stab 'em, and slash 'em apart. You'll get the satisfying feeling and that good *sluck* sound you get when you tear into an enemy's torso. Break ranks! Attack!"

Not a man hesitated, but not a one missed out of the corner of his eye that I was in the thick of the melee, stabbing, slashing, yelling. When they were done, not one whole melon was left in the stake-body.

With seeds and slush and juice all over me and sitting on the tailgate of the truck, I addressed the troops. "I heard that word got out there'd be a picnic today. Well, eat all you want! But don't think of it as watermelon. That's your enemy there, bloody and beaten."

They dug in.

Fanny Wright was a happy intern. Her face smudged with old ink from old newspapers and wearing a big smile, she looked like a clown. I found her in case prep. Spread across one of the tables were photocopies of dozens of disinterred news clips. "It's like the mother lode!" she declared brightly. "I've come out of the cave—the mine shaft—with some nuggets that ought to assay pretty good."

"I'm proud of you, Fanny. Let me take a look."

Fanny took me through the clips—the developer who lost a bundle when Mayor Swinton denied a conditional use for 112 acres of land with highway frontage, the rival banker whom Swinton blocked from opening a motor teller on Main Street, the American Legion post commander whose lucrative bingo operations were halted. There were others, but these three were prime, partly because there were threats of retaliation by the offended parties.

"Now the letters to the editor. Some of these really sizzle. As you said, Swinton was one unpopular s.o.b."

"Were those my exact words?"

Fanny was puzzled.

"Never mind," I said, thinking with amusement how the law enforcement vocabulary, even of a young woman, grew quickly in color, salt, and downright vulgarity. "Let's don't get into the letters. They'll complicate things."

"But there's one . . ."

Deputy Green hustled into case prep.

"Look at this, Marvin," I said. "Just off-hand, would you find a developer, a banker, or a bingo operator more suspicious?"

"Throw in a lawyer, make it easy."

"Swinton went out of his way to avoid taking on lawyers. It was his style not to start something with anybody who could fight back."

Marvin's recollections were nudged alive when he glanced at the clips. The developer, he recalled, had been particularly vehement in his threats against Swinton. Besides, the developer had a history of physical confrontations. He didn't have a record but probably had narrowly escaped arrest more than once.

"That's the hottest one. He claimed he lost $15 million or so 'cause of what Swinton did. The land's still sitting there. Joseph C. Gayette is broke. It's not only motive, it's something that didn't go away."

"I tend to agree with you on that. Course we'll look at all three of them, but make Gayette your number one."

"Sheriff." The intern had been ignored while us old pros conversed. "Sheriff, at least look at one of these letters to the editor. It's got a strange ring to it." Fanny pushed a single letter in front of me.

I read aloud. Marvin's eyes narrowed as he listened.

"As Mayor you single-handedly blocked the low-cost housing project. I and others have spoken and written at length about the way the project could change lives for the better. No more of that. Instead, let us count the cost of your deed. Let us consider the iniquity of your heartless opposition. Families will continue to live in squalor, placing children in peril. Some will live lives of crime. Others will be victims of crime. Some will die before they are grown. Their blood will be on your hands. What you had better think about are the words of Richard Daley in Chicago at the time of the 1968 Democratic Convention."

I looked at Fanny. "So where's the smoking gun?"

"There's a reference to death," Marvin said, "where it says 'some will die.' But that's an accusation, not a threat."

You could tell Fanny was proud of herself. "You guys missed the Richard Daley reference."

"I never knew the mayor of Chicago was any social reformer," I said.

"That's not it. In more than one criminal justice course at Sam Houston State, Daley was quoted. His words have become a standard piece in law enforcement tradition, not as doctrine necessarily, but as a provocative benchmark, or something like that."

"What did the sonofabitch say?" Marvin asked.

"Just three words."

Fanny paused to heighten the drama.

"Shoot to kill."

Marvin and I were impressed with our little intern, but we didn't know exactly why. Instead of asking her what it meant, we both looked thoughtful. Marvin straightened his badge.

"Yeah..." Marvin finally said.

It finally came to me. "He was making a threat, disguised so it would get in the paper. We know that Swinton read a lot, and he would have been..."

"The word is 'voracious.'"

"...would have been a voracious reader of all that Daley did in '68. Daley was a 'tough mayor' role model for Swinton. The letter writer would have known this, too. He didn't write that letter for the editor, or the readers. He wrote a message to Swinton, one that Swinton would recognize."

Something clicked for me at my own last remark. I struggled to make the connection while trying to continue to listen.

"Who is the writer of the letter?" Fanny asked Marvin. "Does this name mean anything to you?"

"Alexander Meredith," Marvin read aloud. "Just rings a vague bell, that's all. I don't know. Let's get Pepys in here."

"I've got it!" I said.

"You know Meredith?"

"No, I mean the note. As I said, the letter was a message to Swinton. So was the note taped to the lavatory. It was not a message to us. The murderer knew that Swinton would die slowly after a shot to the abdomen. In the position he fell, he couldn't miss seeing the note. As he died, he would know who killed him when he read, 'Greetings from Gropius.'"

I felt a thrill of discovery. "I'll get Pepys in here."

Marvin filled Pepys in as they made their way back to case prep. Nodding to Fanny and me, she picked up the letter to the editor, reading it quickly. Then she scanned the three news articles.

"Alexander Meredith retired and moved here ten years ago," she told us. "You're not much aware of him because he hasn't done much here, at least not publicly. Hardly anybody knows how he made his money, which is not inconsiderable. I didn't know myself until his next-door neighbor told Susie, you know Susie does my hair, and Susie told me. That was a few years ago."

"So what was his line of work?" I asked.

"Why, honey, he was an architect."

Chapter Seven

ALEXANDER Meredith was about to become better known in Gilgal. I sent Pepys to update the gossip line however she could and sent Fanny back to the paper office to narrow her search to any other letters Meredith might have written and news items, if any, in which he figured.

Energized by our discoveries, I was eager to get on with the chase, able at least for now to put aside my preoccupation with my own family background. For the first time since the murder, my curiosity was intense. How had the shot been fired into living quarters locked from the inside, a place with no win...

"Marvin! You remember something odd about Swinton's living quarters? No windows along one side. Let's get over there."

Back at the site, we observed as we approached the entry why there were no windows on one side: an attached garage running the length of the wall. There was no direct entry from garage to house;

instead there was a sheltered walkway leading out of the garage and then along to the front entry of the residence.

We entered the garage. Toward the left rear, along the wall opposite where the bathroom would be, I found what I expected. When the lavatory had been raised, the carpenter fashioned an access panel. Marvin removed four screws and detached the panel, revealing the water pipes and the drain. As I shined a flash inside, we saw four screws retaining the inside panel beneath the lavatory. Marvin unscrewed them and pulled that panel away.

"A straight shot to Swinton's belly," I said.

"Yeah," said Marvin. "Then you replace two small panels and eight screws and you've got the perfect crime. Old Swinton thought he was hidden away and protected by alarms, but every time he went to that lavatory it was like standing in public."

"Not the public. Just the guy who knew how to peer through the palisade and wanted to. Not the carpenter, that's my guess, or the plumber, but find out who they were and trace through them. One of them must've told Meredith about it."

After Marvin put the wall back together, we left without entering the house.

It didn't take long for Pepys to learn the names of the plumber and the carpenter. They were brothers, Nathan and Lon Osborne. Lon was the carpenter and the one I talked to.

"For a year or two, I had coffee with Alex at the Fiesta Cafe," Lon told me. "Somewhere along there he told me he was an architect. He had always done big industrial jobs, but he took interest in the least little things having to do with construction. Gave me somebody to talk to about stuff nobody else gave a damn about.

"That lavatory job was a funny one. I had never worked on anything like it. Mostly I was telling him about what Nathan did, because that was the funny part, putting that little lavatory up at chest level. As usual, Alex wanted to know every detail, and that's when I went on and told him about the access panel. That was the part I did, didn't do anything with the pipes, that was Nathan. You don't have any proof Alex did the shooting, do you? Just because he knew how to see in there don't mean he did it. I don't want him to be in trouble on account of me, but you asked me, and I figured I had to tell you."

I needed one more thing. There were several items I didn't have, like the murder weapon, but there was this one thing I thought I needed. It was the influence of Benjamin Edes, I knew, that led me in this direction. I would have liked to get the object before I even talked to Alexander Meredith, certainly before I came close to charging him, but that was not possible. I had to go to a judge for a search warrant in order to find what I was after, and for that I would have to build some kind of case.

What I had on motive was flimsy. I put together what I could.

I could show that opportunity was virtually Meredith's alone, assuming he had no alibi for the time of the murder.

Judge Mancill, more puzzled than exasperated, issued the search warrant for Meredith's residence.

People just didn't seem to care that I had a major murder case on my hands. They went right on with their own trifles, and, the bad part was, wanted me in on them. My thoughts went something like this after I hung up the telephone from talking with Jake Gordon, one of Gilgal's few Jewish residents.

The carillon at the Methodist Church, just outside the Gilgal jurisdiction, could be heard a mile or so away, even across the river that ran on the other side of town. Jake lived a lot closer than that. He didn't mind the midday playing of hymns at all, Jake said. That wasn't his complaint. That they were Protestant hymns was not his complaint, either. In fact, he rather enjoyed them and looked forward to them. His complaint was that he had just heard them playing the Nazi anthem, "Deutschland Uber Alles."

The sheriff of all of Joshua County, Texas, was not the one to call for something like this. If you wanted it stopped, you could ask a judge for an injunction. If the judge granted it, you could then get me to enforce it. In fact, a low key conversation with the Methodist minister would probably resolve it. But folks didn't see it this way. The sheriff was their protector, their mediator, their detention hall monitor. In Jake's case, he was an avid supporter who had made generous campaign contributions to me. I got in my car and headed to pay a call on The Reverend Meleen.

"If you can't show up on Sundays, not even on Easter, I'm glad to see you in the house of the Lord on a weekday, Cable." Then he was mighty puzzled when told the reason for the visit. "Well, that just can't be. We wouldn't play that. Truth is, the music is on tapes. No one here in the church selects it. We don't even know what's going to be on until we hear it ourselves. But we get the tapes from the church outfit in Nashville. I don't believe there's any way it could be on there."

I wished now I had brought Jake with me. Maybe Jake could hum a little bit of it. No, that wouldn't be possible, I realized. Humming it would be even more distasteful for Jake than hearing it piped over the carillon.

"I can hum it," The Reverend Meleen offered. "I was a history major as an undergraduate, before going to seminary. In one course we were exposed to Nazi culture, the movies, the music. I rather took a fancy to that piece, I hate to admit. And I just sort of naturally remember a good tune once I've heard it played. Dah, dah dah dah, dah dah, dah-dah-dah; dah dah, dah dah, dah dah-dah-dah."

The choir director, Knowles Shaw, passing by, stopped and stuck his head in the door. "You've solved my problem! I was trying to think of just the right hymn for a place on the Sunday program. That's it! We haven't done that in a long time."

"You've ever done it? I mean, you have done that here in this church?" asked the pastor.

The director now spotted me. I felt something must be going past me.

"Of course we've done it, but as I say, not in a long time."

"What is the name of it?" asked the pastor.

"Glorious Things of Thee Are Spoken."

They went to the reference books. "Look at this," said the director. "A Croatian folk song provided the melody for the Austrian national anthem in an arrangement by Franz Joseph Haydn in 1797. It goes on to say that in the church the same tune was used with the words, John Newton's 1779 words, of 'Glorious Things of Thee Are Spoken,' as well as twenty or so other lyrics."

I would report back to Jake Gordon and suggest

that Jake, the Reverend Meleen, and the choir director get together to discuss it. Maybe something ecumenical would come of it.

Then I drove by O. B.'s place to report to him, just for the sport of it. As usual, O. B. was a step ahead of me. "You've come to arrest me, for my part in getting 'Deutschland Uber Alles' beamed all over Joshua County?"

"Just rounding up the usual suspects," was my rejoinder.

"And I'm a suspect because I've often told you I fought on the wrong side in the last war." O. B. had fought in B-29s in the Pacific theatre during World War II.

I related how the mystery had been solved, much to O. B.'s delight. "How can use of the melody by Nazis in later days outweigh centuries of church music tradition?" he asked me. "Does it make sense to add it to the growing contemporary *Index* of proscribed banners, anecdotes, and other songs?"

"O. B., you surprise me with how much you know about so many things."

"All that I've learned, I've forgotten. The little that I still know, I've guessed. The French aphorist Chamford said that. I wish I had. Anyway, you want to know something about music, you should ask me."

I knew that to be the truth. The string bass player and erstwhile B-29 flyer, with whom I now spoke, had been touring with a small band in the years after the war. The drummer didn't show up one night. Their performance was in a small town, where no substitute drummer could be found. After looking, the band leader said to his bass player, "No drummer tonight. You'll have to keep us on meter all by yourself. Looks like you're the only beat in town."

O. B., for "only beat," was his sobriquet from then on.

"Cable, you still seeing that woman, what's her name, Linda Faye, works at the map factory?"

"Still am. What about you? Dating anybody?"

"Some. I'm not choosy. All I insist on is, I want a clean woman."

"Washed with Ivory soap?"

"No, a woman who has stood naked in a light rain."

Marvin had not easily traced the provenance of the diamonds that had been found in the Trans Am from the Equal Opportunity Car Lot. For one thing, he was pressed in pursuing evidence in the Swinton murder case. For another, he had to begin by obtaining a technical description of the stones. It wasn't enough to ask if anyone had reported x-number of diamonds missing.

Colleagues in law enforcement in Texas had been of little help. Even in Fort Worth and Dallas and Houston there were not enough jewel thefts to warrant having a specialist on the force. A Tarrant County deputy did tell him he had once called on the services of an appraiser in San Antonio, and gave Marvin the name and address.

Dayton Loos, located on Presa Street, did not drive and resisted the idea of traveling at all. Marvin, with extreme reluctance, planned a trip to San Antonio. Taking Deputy Jack Redwine to ride shotgun, he stowed the cache in the trunk of his Dodge Intrepid and headed east on I-10.

As meticulous and as compulsive as he was,

Marvin had made a day's work out of deciding whether to put the diamonds in the trunk or to keep them constantly in his sight, on the seat between him and Redwine. The trunk finally won. He weighed, too, the relative merits of wearing his uniform or plainclothes. The uniform finally won.

He had gotten the appraiser to schedule the whole day for the job. Marvin could not tolerate an overnight, guarding the diamonds.

With much relief he pulled into a private parking spot just off Presa right at the jeweler's back entrance. Deputy Redwine alit first and stood with gun drawn as Marvin unlocked the trunk, took out the booty, still in the Old No. 7 tin, and hurried through the door being held open, as prearranged, by Loos.

Also open, a few feet inside, was the vault. Marvin strode quickly into its safety with Redwine and Loos at his heels.

Loos stayed at it all day. At a few minutes past 6 pm, he handed Marvin the inventory, prepared with the help of a computer program that had some basic jewel descriptions in memory. "What you've got here comes to $778,000 wholesale, way I figure it."

Marvin thanked Loos, asked him to send his bill to the Joshua County Sheriff's Office, and didn't waste any time getting out of the vault and out of the building, guarded by Jack Redwine as he had been upon entering. Marvin breathed a big, audible sigh of relief when he closed the trunk of the Intrepid, the tin of diamonds safely inside.

The trip back up I-10 to Gilgal went without incident. When the jewels were again secure in the sheriff's office safe, Marvin quickly found me, gave me a report, and said, "I've gotta have a drink."

We also got a bite to eat at the Fiesta Cafe; then

Marvin headed back to the courthouse and sat down at his terminal. He had reflected during the drive to San Antonio that he did not want to disclose detailed descriptions of the stones. Any claimant would have to provide specs in order to make a successful retrieval of his property.

As he worked the net, he made a discovery that would obviate any need to post descriptions at all. Uncommonly high activity among several diamond dealers during a period of a couple of weeks several months ago was noted. Marvin couldn't figure out what it meant, but he knew it meant something. He would talk with me the next morning.

I listened, frowning in concentration. I had looked at the jeweler's inventory, stone by stone. "You know what this could mean, Marvin? We may not be dealing with stolen property at all. Get Warren Bacon in the interrogation room. I'm gonna grill him good."

Bacon had healed some, but my rough handling of him in the shed was hot on his mind. I sensed this from the look on Bacon's face, even the tenseness evident in his shoulders and arms. I guessed I wouldn't have to lay a hand on him.

"Okay, boy, save yourself some pain. Lay it all out for us. We've figured out what you did. Just fill in the names and dates for us."

Bacon moved in his chair, jerking himself to one side.

I waited. I managed a benevolent look on my face.

Bacon tried, "You don't know anything."

I frowned and waited.

"I was just sent for those rocks. I don't even know anything about it myself."

"That's not quite right. But I'm glad you're cooperating. Tell me about the drug dealer."

"I'm not in here on any drug charge! Look at my rap sheet. I've never dealt drugs."

I knew that was true. "It was a double money laundry. The kingpin got uneasy when he read in the papers about the investigation of the Houston banks. He laundered the drug income in this country, through the banks as usual. Then came the second part of the double laundry. He bought diamonds with the cash, and hired you to take them to him in Mexico. Where did you fuck up, Bacon?"

I could see Bacon beginning to crumble. *He'll soon be Bacon bits.*

I had done no more than lay out for Bacon the hypothesis I had formed. I had hit the nail on the head. Bacon was convinced that I did in fact know just about everything that had gone on. He began to pour it out.

"I never have sold drugs, bought drugs, used drugs. I was paid to deliver a message in an envelope. I knew it was going to the kingpin in Mexico, but I thought what the hell, it's only a message. The pay was good, half up front and the other half when I made the delivery.

"My Trans Am was ten years old. With that half-payment in hand, I traded it in on a new one. I drove in style to the cartel drop. They took the envelope with the message in it and then put me in a little room. It wasn't long until they dragged me out of there, damn near broke my neck.

"'What you trying to pull?' they asked me. They had looked for the weld spot in the frame. See, they put those diamonds in there back when they hired me, while they made sure I was with them and away from the car for half a day. That way I wouldn't know what I was transporting. Just a message, I was told. Just a message, I thought.

"Because they could see the new Trans Am sitting right there, and because they could see I wasn't running in the other direction, I was able to convince them what I had done. 'Get the fucking diamonds,' they told me.

"When I went back to the dealer and found the car had been sold at an auction lot, I traced it to this car lot here in Gilgal. I would have bought it back, but I had just paid for the new one and was strapped for cash. I had to move quick, with the drug mob breathing on me. That's why I stole it. I was going to take it back."

I sat there. I myself had not been able to guess how the car mix-up had occurred. The revelation was simple once you heard it, and I sat there and marveled at it. My marveling done, I called to Marvin. "Come get him."

To Bacon I said, "Even a sorry bastard like you has got something coming to him for cooperating. You're in here on charges of car theft and battery. I'm not going to charge you with anything else. You'll go to trial. You'll go to the penitentiary, probably a short term. Whether I'm doing you any favor or not depends on how fast you run from your recent employer once you get out."

I got up and left.

A little later I told Marvin, "Go with me. I want you to be there when I tell Lucky the diamonds belong to him. They don't come under the federal confiscatory statute, because they weren't seized in a drug raid and they weren't even in the possession of a drug dealer. You and I haven't proved, either, that they are the property of a drug kingpin; we just have the word of a thief on that. I would say the kingpin did a damn good double-laundering job. For Lucky and the Equal Opportunity Car Lot, those stones are clean."

Chapter Eight

I have to guess, with only a little physical evidence thrown in, about what the stalker was doing as he tracked me. As I reflect on his actions now, knowing now what eventually happened, I think of him as a wily raptor, secretive and determined.

The raptor first had to make sure of his target. He could not risk asking questions in Gilgal, or Joshua County, or even in adjoining counties. He didn't stay in the area but instead made forays in his pick-up. He did not want to be recognized at all. The truck was a Ford, not a new model, not noticeably old, just a pick-up like thousands of others that were part of the Lone Star landscape.

He mostly relied upon overheard conversations. Having a beer or sipping a cup of java, he would tune in on chatter at the bar or a nearby table. My re-election proved to be the raptor's big break. Even beyond adjoining counties I was known and my doings were followed, particularly by old-timers who knew I was the scion of old Banner. This connection was the one the raptor needed. "Old Banner's grandboy has won his race," the raptor heard. He concentrated, shutting out other talk, and tried to pick up more. In the day or so before the election result in Joshua County was old news in the hinterlands, the raptor became satisfied by what he put together from scraps of talk.

It was the way he had learned to live, on the sly, on the fly. He headed for Gilgal. For his prey to turn out to be a sheriff was good and it was bad. On the bad side, a lawman might have some skills. He might not; all you had do to get the job was get elected. Finding me alone might be a problem, with me being in the company of deputies, law from other agencies, and people in general.

On the good side, he knew where to start the tail. A sheriff had to show up at his office, and he had to depart. On his first day in Gilgal after the election, the raptor used this vector to follow me to my apartment, just noting its location and moving on. It was later that same night he was standing near Lady Banksia, soaking in what he could and hoping for a good close view of the his prey. He had to know what I looked like if he was going to take me. His hope was not rewarded. It would be another day when he saw the object of his hunt, saw me up close, when by chance he brushed up against me when passing me on a sidewalk in downtown Gilgal. The chance encounter made little impression on me at the time, but he was a stranger with an unusual look about him and later I was able to recall the incident and recall him.

My hopes not high, I took along Marvin and

another deputy to look for the weapon. Fanny came with us to help with the search for other prime evidence. A letter to the editor containing a cryptic death threat, published several years ago, was a weak reed to support motive for murder. I was assuming a noble passion grounded in the Bauhaus movement and modernism. A noble passion, I thought, *that's the worst kind.*

Amongst Meredith's books might be found tinder that fueled his passion. In his own diaries and writings, if any, might be found flames of expression. To bolster evidence of motive was my primary purpose in the search of Meredith's possessions.

I had put a tail on Meredith just long enough to determine that he seemed always to remain at his residence, where he lived alone, until almost noon. I showed up at nine with Marvin at my side. The other deputy and Fanny stayed outside. Marvin and I followed the architect into his large, comfortable study. I would not hand Meredith the search warrant until the questioning ended.

Alexander Meredith was relaxed, even nonchalant. It was an aplomb that would not be shaken. Following the usual introductory explanations, I told Meredith I believed there were some things about the victim that Meredith might know that could be helpful. Did he know, for example, that the late Phil G. Swinton had gotten a lavatory installed at custom height?

"Surely, Sheriff Bannerman, you do not expect that I would know a trivial detail like that about anyone in Gilgal, much less a man I so detested?"

I noted that Meredith had not denied knowledge

but had, in fact, just countered a question with a question. Still, it amounted to a lie.

"Did you detest Swinton enough to murder him?"

"To say I detested him would not be tantamount to saying I commited murder."

Not a denial.

"Do you know of anybody who did hate him enough to kill him?"

"Their numbers are legion. This was not a likeable man who recently met his Maker; surely you know that, Sheriff Bannerman."

"Would you give me a name or two?"

"Of course I will give you no name. The late Mr. Swinton offended many of his fellow citizens, both as an officious banker and an insensitive mayor. I merely speak in generalities when I agree with you that scores of people wished him dead."

I had said nothing like that.

"Merely generalities. I was far from being on close enough terms with him to know how he may have driven someone into a rage, inciting that someone to put an end to his sorry life. Murders usually are traced to that kind of thing, are they not? Rages? Even disagreements with close kin?"

"What about reaction against him for things he did as mayor, as you mentioned, Alex?" I was not going to be drawn into the formality of address evidently preferred by Mr. Meredith.

"Not just things he did, Sheriff Bannerman, things he said. He could hurt large numbers of people just by opening his mouth. He was an ass."

I looked at Meredith.

Meredith looked at me.

"You have no reputation for diffidence, Sheriff Bannerman, so why do you so obliquely pursue a line of inquiry that is meant to lead inexorably to my very public contention with the late mayor concerning low-cost housing? Why do you not ask me directly rather than erecting an elaborate pretense that somehow I 'might know things about the victim that could be helpful'?"

By now, I could see, the architect had surmised that it was the several-years-old letter to the editor in *Harry's of the West* that had prompted my visit. For Fanny and Marvin and me the discovery had been an exciting retrieval of something lost, a forgotten letter in dusty archives. For Meredith, the letter was not lost at all. Although several years had passed, in his mind it had been penned only yesterday, was still fresh in his mind, and was not something it would even occur to him to deny.

"All right, Alex, has the mayor's opposition to low-cost housing festered in your mind, causing you finally to punish him?"

I thought I saw a fleeting gleam of satisfaction in Meredith's eyes at his use of the word 'punish.'

"Things do not 'fester' in my mind, Sheriff Bannerman. Things form in my mind, are analyzed in my mind, and are sorted in my mind."

I decided to cut the questioning short and get on with the search of the premises.

"Tell me, Alex, do you have stored in your mind a precise recollection of where you were Wednesday night, November the seventh?"

"Indeed I do. As little as I care for watching television, there was that evening an A&E presentation to which I had looked forward. I put it on my calendar, and at the appointed hour I watched it. Here. In my residence."

"Was anyone here with you?"

"Not a living soul."

Meredith continued to speak with the same indulgent good humor with which he had begun.

An answer but not an alibi, I thought. I knew I could follow with more questions to good profit, but now was not the time.

"I appreciate it, Alex, I appreciate talking with you." Producing the warrant, I said, "Marvin will get you to give him a handwriting sample. I'll need to take a look through your place here, and I know . . ."

"That it's an intrusion? But you're an intruder, that's your profession. So go ahead. Do be careful with my things. I have seen no mention in the paper of the discovery of the murder weapon. So you must see if it can be discovered here. So do proceed to see if you may discover the knife, the rope, the wrench, the revolver, or whatever it may have been."

A little earlier, on a silent cue from me, Marvin had slipped out long enough to motion to Fanny and the deputy. They now entered and our team of four began searching.

No weapon was found, no firearm of any kind. Fanny stifled an outcry of delight when she came upon a slim volume in Meredith's library. It was *Night of January 16th*, a play by Ayn Rand.

I had rounded up Marvin and the other deputy and came to the library to see if Fanny was done. "You won't believe this!" she whispered to me. "I'll explain after we get out of here, but can you bag it as evidence now?"

Taking Fanny at her word, I said nothing but slipped the Ayn Rand play into a pouch. I wrote a receipt to give to Meredith, then led my entourage to the front porch where the owner had relaxed during the search.

"I see you have found the murder weapon," he told me as he accepted the receipt. "Beat over the head with a book, was he? That clears me. I would have employed a volume of Edward Gibbon's *Decline and Fall of the Roman Empire,* or perhaps the whole boxed set. Considerably more heft than *Night of January 16th,* you know. Or merely required him to read every word of *Decline and Fall.* Many have found that to be a killing task."

How do you reply to something like that, when spoken by a murder suspect?

I murmured a word of appreciation for the patience Meredith had shown, and my team and I left the porch.

Fanny explained, as the other three of us huddled with her next to the patrol car and listened raptly, that *Night of January 16th* was obscure and rarely if ever mentioned by Rand's enthusiasts. It laid bare what Rand's 'objectivism' really meant. Anarchy, of course. In particular, she told them, the play provided a rationale for murder for anyone who chose to commit it.

"Fanny, that little play is a priceless find. In my mind, it's incriminating. In a court of law, it proves little. It would be no more than a thin shred along with other circumstantial evidence. Here's its value: in grilling Meredith. The architect is going to have to convict himself."

Chapter Nine

THAT night, I went to bed puzzled. Next morning I woke up puzzled. Why wasn't I fierce in my zeal to nail Alexander Meredith? Why wasn't I maybe even fantasizing about some bizarre move by the suspect that would give me an opening to shoot Meredith dead, *mano a mano*? Here I was, on my quest to justify why I felt so prone to violence in handling criminals, and right now I didn't even feel that way. Had the fellow charmed me? Had I come to think it was a pretty good thing that the elegant and witty Meredith had punished that sorry s.o.b. Swinton?

I stopped first at the paper office. I had an obligation to tell Benjamin Edes of progress in the Swinton case.

Ben was intrigued by Meredith as prime suspect and particularly taken with the idea of Rand's *Night of January 16th* as incriminating evidence. That a letter published in *Harry's of the West* had pointed a finger at the architect was icing on the cake. With no prodding from me, talk did turn to my favorite subject.

"How's your reading coming?"

I told Ben of my urge to get directly to the matter, my recent visit to the ranch, and my hope that Dooley Charter would indeed reveal some key to my family history.

Ben Edes had already recognized my impatience with the regimen of reading. As I learned later, Ben had put his repertorial skills to work and had pried out of Dooley Charter the story that I myself had been unable to ferret. "It's yours to reveal," Ben had told Dooley. "Think on it, and when you can bring yourself to do it, tell Cable what happened." Dooley didn't say yea or nay. Ben kept his own counsel and said nothing to me.

Ben was silent for a few moments, pondering what he had learned about me from Dooley and his entreaty to Dooley to tell me. Finally he decided to dissemble. "That's all well and good, Cable, but as enticing as a piece of the real world is to you, it's worthless out of context, and the context is literature."

"I'm reading, for God's sake, but you *live* life, that's how you learn."

"Men lived life for centuries before there was language and didn't learn a damn thing. If there were no language, still just grunts, we wouldn't even be having this conversation."

"You sure as hell wouldn't be a newspaper editor."

"Speaking of which, let me show you this letter I've received for publication."

I read the letter, whose burden was to show that words lose their meaning over the years, with an attendant loss in public morals. It closed with the line, "We have to keep our eye on words."

"What do you think, Cable? Should I publish this letter from Ward Allen? And don't answer as some of my readers would. About half of them think they're smarter than everybody else. They'll read a complicated piece and tell me that none of my other readers will understand it."

"I'm surprised you would want to publish it, a strong conservative letter like that."

"I'm no liberal, Cable. A moderate perhaps, and around here that passes for liberal, or worse. But particularly in matters of language, I'm of the old school. I'm going to put it in tomorrow's paper."

"That'll send a lot of your readers to the dictionary. I hope some of them have a copy of Horatio's *Unabridged Dictionary*."

Ben chuckled at the unexpected jest from me. "Cable, let me ask you, do we consider language important in the sense Ward Allen summons in this letter, or do we just accept the usefulness of language for giving orders, as you do, or getting out a paper, as I do, and cut if off there? And refuse to go any further? Listen, Cable, from literature you learn psychology."

Ben paused, looking into me.

"I see the reluctance in your face, but you don't learn psychology from psychologists, who mostly are absorbed in abnormal psychology, leaving aside Erich Fromm. Did you ever hear your literature professors mention a psychologist by name?"

"Well…"

"Jung! That's the one they all mention. There's a reason for it. Jung leaves open the door to mystery, even opens it wider. Literary people like that. Novelists in particular like it. They like to believe there's magic in the world."

"I don't remember that magic was all that big at A & M."

"You just took the required courses, and they're all mass-produced. Maybe you didn't hear any mention of Jung. They mostly put graduate teaching assistants in those slots. I don't know if it's worse to be taught by full profs, who're tired of it all, or TAs, green but at least naively intellectually energetic. It's not all bad to be a naif."

"Where are you taking me with all this?"

"One never knows. One night I told Madison and Budge and Sara—I've mentioned them to you before—I told Madison and them, when they were tight…"

"They weren't tight; *you* were tight."

"Yes, well, I told of my idea of *l'autre monde*, a unifying theory of such conceptual power that it could, in just a few words, connect and explain all of literature, psychology, philosophy, and educational theory."

"Now I *know* you were tight."

"I had worked it out when sober. I really had something. But since that night, I never have been able to put it all back together."

"Sounds like Humpty Dumpty *monde*."

"Speaking of Madison Jones, I should tell you to read him. You'd learn how people are fated to behave as they behave, fated by the deeds of previous generations, fated by the creeds passed down, fated by the very land around them. That's different, by the way, from Faulkner's notion of a 'curse' on the land and the people, and certainly more plausible than Faulkner in a scientific age. I realize what I'm saying may seem to contradict what I said about novelists and Jung and magic, but believe me, there's magic enough in Madison Jones. Anyway, that's your kind of stuff, Cable."

"Sounds like it."

"I would tell you to read Oxford Stroud, too, except that it would not help you understand anything. Even Stroud does not understand Stroud."

I left the paper office intellectually invigorated. Upon reflection, however, I was at a loss to pinpoint a single useful thing I had learned.

Arriving at the courthouse, I strode through my office without even checking my calls or in-basket and went straight in to case prep. Marvin was already there.

"I've got a report back from the handwriting lab. The Gropius note is a solid match. Meredith lettered it in that near-perfect style that architects use, but of course there are still personal characteristics."

Did Meredith want to be known as the punisher of Swinton? Had he been over-confident? Or had he just gotten careless?

"We've nailed him, Marvin. Even in the absence of the murder weapon, we've placed him at the scene. Go get him, I want him in here for questioning. Arrest him for the murder, then bring him in."

Alexander Meredith's pride made him forego his right to have an attorney present. His first reply to my grilling made him appear to be well-represented.

"Of course I penned the note. What could you be thinking, Sheriff Bannerman? I stuck it on a package I sent him some time ago. A gift. A gift meant to shame him, a gag, you might say, except that I was deadly serious about it. I gave him a rusty skeleton key with a tag saying, 'A key to your perfect world, you stingy bastard.' You can see he saved the note, then used it to incriminate me. Maybe it was suicide after all, Sheriff Bannerman. Go look for another architectural marvel, a trap-door through which he dropped a gun after fatally wounding himself. Or perhaps someone else did it and taped the note to the lavatory."

"You expect me to believe this?"

"Go find the skeleton key."

Marvin straightened his badge.

I made an effort to keep a poker face. Why hadn't I thought of this?

Alexander Meredith relaxed in the large leather chair. Marvin raced to the Swinton place. With little effort he found the key on Swinton's desk, displayed evidently with some pleasure. Just like the bastard.

Back in case prep, Marvin carefully, even ostentatiously, placed the rusty old key on the table in front of where I stood. Still attached to it was the "stingy bastard" tag.

Marvin let my dismay sink in, then show on my face and in the sag of my frame.

More carefully, more ostentatiously, Marvin now placed beside the key and tag a neatly lettered card.

I looked at it. I read the lettering. Now I wanted to kill. I wanted to kill Marvin. I grinned at the deputy. Phil G. Swinton had saved the original, kept it on his desk tucked under the skeleton key. It said, "Greetings from Gropius."

Marvin and I went into the office where Meredith still sat comfortably in the leather chair. I told him of the discovery of the original card, saved by Swinton and not taped to the lavatory. "Mr. Alexander Meredith," I said, now enjoying the formality, "you will want to call a lawyer, to try to arrange bail.

Deputy Marvin Green will be taking you to a cell in the jail."

Meredith kept his composure but good humor left his face. "Perhaps you are right, Sheriff Bannerman. Please call my attorney, Gideon Lincecum, for me."

Chapter Ten

I have reconstructed what must have been happening. Ready now to make his move, the raptor slowly pulled his truck away from the curb a block back from where he saw my patrol car exit the courthouse parking lot. In the dusk, he had to keep an eye on my rear lights, fairly distinctive in his mind by now, to avoid letting me slip out of sight.

Luck was with him. My car was traveling the streets and making the turns that would lead to the offices of *Harry's of the West*. That's where the snare would be set.

Benjamin Edes had bought a large, handsome old residence near the bank of the river that ran through Gilgal and had converted it into the newspaper's building. The huge basement, floored with concrete, adapted perfectly to the press room. Entrance to a below-ground loading dock area was to the rear where the river ran. Edes's office, the newsroom, advertising, layout and composing, and business offices were on the main floor. The upper floor housed a spacious library, a conference room, and a space for cooking and snacking.

The grounds covered close to two acres and accommodated an abundance of trees, flowers, and shrubbery. Neatly tended for the most part, the foliage tangled into something of a thicket on the side toward the river.

I pulled in at my favorite place, not easily visible from the street, near the loading dock, and went to Ben's office.

"As Housman commented, 'The passion for truth is the faintest of human emotions.' It burns bright in you at times, Cable. I'm glad you dropped by."

I acknowledged the warm welcome. "I'm reading an Agatha Christie mystery, *The Sleeping Murder*. There's a line, 'Leave the past alone.' Maybe that's what I should do." I said no more, sensing that Ben had been deep in thought and was pleased now to come to the surface and talk out loud to somebody.

"This whole country has long had a theme park mentality, a phenomenon that predates Disney by centuries. In Alabama, in 1836, a 15-year-old girl, Lizzie Taylor, led a town to be named. She had been reading an Oliver Goldsmith poem, and her fancy was caught by the line, 'Sweet Auburn! loveliest village of the plain.' She suggested to her sweetheart's daddy, the founder, that the new town be named Auburn, and so it was."

Sometimes Ben spoke as if he were working out an editorial in his mind, and more than once I had indeed seen in print the same thoughts Ben had recently expressed to me in conversation.

"Later, a college was established there. Now take note, this was a land of rolling hills, fairly rocky in spots, mostly forested. No plains in sight! But at the college some fans called the athletic teams 'the Plainsmen.' They named the school paper the *Auburn Plainsman*. Get it? It was a theme. The theme simply came from a poem, a few lines on paper, and the whim of a girl, and had nothing to do with the reality of the place!"

"Why are you so worked up over this, Ben?"

"It has to do with thoughts and words. Thoughts matter. Words matter."

"Do theme parks matter?"

"Not to me they don't. What Goldsmith's poem was really about was a sad thing that happened to a town in England. The name of the poem was 'The Deserted Village.' The principal point, however, has been ignored on the 'plains' in Alabama because it's not pretty. Of course there is 'village this' and 'village that.' If the population of Auburn should grow to a million, they'll still call it a village, because that's the theme.

"Once started, a theme never stops. A faculty member in recent times was there for twenty-five years. On the side he fancied himself an entertainer, an impresario, and a *namer of things*. He named novels; he named awards; he named all sorts of things. In all that time he never managed to accomplish anything important enough to warrant a mention in the history of Auburn, except—get this, Cable—except he named a choral group 'The Oliver Goldsmith Singers.' That won him a place in Simms and Logue's *Pictorial History of Auburn*."

"Could we talk about Joshua County a little bit, Ben?"

"That's what I'm getting to. A pioneer in the 1840s stopped his wagons at a creek over in the next county. He declared to his family that he was going to name the creek after himself. They called him 'Big Joshua' to distinguish him from his son, also named Joshua.

"'Papa,' the boy said, 'I sure would like a creek named after me.'

"'There are lots of creeks in the Texas hill country, son. I'll wait for mine. This one we'll call 'Little Joshua Creek.'

"The next one they came to, he named 'Big Joshua Creek.'

"To this day, people are mystified when they see that Little Joshua Creek is bigger than Big Joshua Creek.

"Then they traveled on here, and Joshua founded this county and got it named after him. There was nothing Biblical about it, see? Except his name had come from the Bible. But theme fever soon struck. Later settlers gave the name Gilgal to the county seat. Soon an anecdote was concocted: A stranger asks, 'Where do you find Gilgal?' 'Why, you find it in Joshua.' Heh heh heh.

"In the present century, the inevitable happened. Reading a footnote in the Bible, a fan learned that 'Gilgal' means 'rolling stone.' That, Cable, is why the Gilgal High School athletic teams are called the Rolling Stones. Before I learned that, I thought it had something to do with William Sydney Porter, you know, O. Henry, who published a paper in Austin with that name.

"There are several little places out in the county with names drawn from the Book of Joshua, too. One of them, Gibeon, is only a crossroads. I'm tempted to spend my own money to erect a road sign there, saying 'Stand still in Gibeon.—Joshua 10:12.' That will delight the theme-parkers. Of course it will mock them, which is my purpose.

"It would mock and offend these amateur Biblicists even more were I to put up signs at the county line saying 'Joshua County, Texas, where prostitution is legal and passing wind is welcome.' There are sources in the Book of Joshua for those statements, also."

"Ben, you support the whole community in your paper, the schools, United Fund, even the churches. How can you say what you're saying?"

"May I not have my own private sardonicism?"

"I guess so."

"Just as in 'the loveliest village,' over in Alabama, the main point of the literary source has been ignored here in this county. The tribes were taking over land, and cities, and the Lord was egging them on, according to their own accounts. They would slaughter the inhabitants, that is, the owners, and take their land and their worldly goods. If what was done around here to the Indians and the Mexicans had been done before the Book of Joshua was written, instead of the other way around, Joshua would be a fit allegory for how this area was settled."

"Sounds like I should read Joshua."

"You should. I don't know why I haven't thought to suggest it. Then you would have better than ranching precedent for the thrill you get in killing; you would have Biblical sanction. There's something else our theme-parkers have never done, because it's not pretty. The Israelites left a reminder of what they had done. Joshua had them set up twelve stones, one for each tribe, in their camp near the Jordan River. There is no monument, no reminder around here of the killing of Indians and mistreatment of Mexicans. There is no reminder of stones."

By the time I returned to my parking place after chatting with Ben, the raptor had had ample time to park a couple of blocks away and carefully sneak to the place of the snare.

The raptor had nerved himself to take a risk, emerge from the brush, and pounce on me right at the door to my car. It worked out better. The raptor watched as I headed not for my car but through the brush toward the river. I was seeking respite at a little grassy place on the bluff overlook. I would be completely alone and unseen, as I wanted to be. My wishes played me right into the raptor's hands.

Beginning to stalk me at the moment I headed toward the river, the raptor had glided silently to a spot right near me. One quick leap and he was at my back, one cord-like forearm pinning my chest and a claw-like hand, gripping a knife, curled around my neck.

"You didn't want to come down here. You wanted to go to your car. Let's go there now." Like an unwilling partner at a dance, I found myself being led back from the river, through the brush, and to a rear door of the sedan.

"Open it," was an order almost spit out.

I complied.

The threat of the knife and the insistence of the forearm had me in the back seat of my own car, behind the wire grill meant to keep a dangerous prisoner at bay. The raptor took cuffs from his belt and fastened me to the grill. A fist to the head knocked me out. Then the raptor opened the front door, got behind the steering wheel, and hit the ignition.

He headed the patrol car in the direction of Bannerman Ranch. About five miles west of Gilgal, I regained consciousness. Pulling myself up as close to the wire as I could, I shouted to the driver, "Who the hell are you?"

"You're talking to the avenging angel, Little Banner. The name is Lammie. That must mean something to you."

It didn't.

"It ought to. It means a lot to me. My brother's name means even more. My brother's name was Jeph Lammie."

I racked my brain, that part of it that was fully conscious. Why was this name supposed to ring a bell with me?

"I'm Horace Lammie." Horace had taken for granted everybody in the Banner family knew the name Jeph Lammie. Over the years they had gloated or laughed. That's what he figured. Now it came to him that, growing up after the incident, Little Banner had never been told anything. That was worse than being laughed about. Jeph had been forgotten.

That I knew nothing seemed to sharpen the raptor's anger. "You've got a price to pay. Too bad you had no say in naming the price, but there it is. Something like thirty years ago, my older brother Jeph signed on at your granddaddy's ranch. He never left that ranch. Know what that means?"

"Doesn't mean a damn thing to me. What are you getting at?"

"He never left because he couldn't leave. He went there and never was seen again. What could I do about it then? Folks like us couldn't do nothing about nothing back then. But I didn't forget my brother. Time came when I could look into it. Never nailed it down, but I know he went there and he never left, and I heard enough, or enough was left out, that there ain't no two ways about it. Jeph was killed on that ranch. Your granddaddy killed him. I had to wait 'til I could give full time to it. I had to work for a living, not like some rancher boy who inherits a whole lot. Well, I waited. Now I'm here. Now you pay."

"What am I paying for?"

"You're paying for something you couldn't help. You're going to pay because you're the only living descendant of Cameron Bannerman I can find, the one what killed my brother. Blood tells, they say. Well, Cameron is long gone, so blood is telling on you. A Bannerman has got to die. You're the Bannerman."

"You could have killed me back there at the river."

"Yeah, I could have killed you. But Jeph didn't die there. I want to see you die where Jeph died. On the great Bannerman Ranch. A practical matter, too, Sheriff. A body at the paper office gets found quick. A body on the great Bannerman Ranch? Well, close to thirty years and nobody's found Jeph. How long you think before they find yours?"

So I was going to meet my end on hallowed ground. On ground where I had been a boy. On ground where I had ridden. On ground where I had been loved.

No, I didn't think so. I leaned back as much as I could, handcuffed, and tried to relax. Tried to think. I conversed no more with Horace Lammie. Instead, I tuned myself for response at the first opportunity. Handcuffs or not, there had to be an opportunity.

We drove on in silence.

As Lammie had planned in his days of scouting, he headed the sedan toward a back entrance to the ranch, miles from the main gate. The deed had to be done on ranch property but in a remote spot where no one would interfere and my corpse would likely remain undiscovered. He pulled the car to a stop. With knife at the ready, he uncuffed me and pulled me out of the back seat, pushing me to my knees.

"This one's for Jeph." Lammie swiped at my cheek with the blade, drawing blood. "There's more to come."

"This one's for Jeph, too." The now bloody knife nicked my bare right arm.

"This one's for me. I ought to get something for my trouble," as the blade ripped down the left side of my shirt, slashing away at flesh. I was bleeding plenty now, my clothes becoming soaked.

At the first cut, I moved my right arm to my side, as if protecting it. Slowly I let my wrist and arm sneak around my upper hip to a spot in the small of my back.

That's where I kept the little derringer. It was old-fashioned. It was quaint. I had taken a lot of ribbing from Marvin and others and never gave up the little pistol. Now I had it. Almost had it. A little more . . . and there! I waited for Lammie's next slash, this one aimed at a leg. The low motion unbalanced Lammie just a little, just enough for me to whip the derringer around and shoot point-blank at Lammie's chest.

The tiny projectile hit home but didn't hit hard, only enough to stun Lammie. He rolled away, regaining his grip on the bloody knife. I had remained in motion after the pistol shot, grabbing a rock I had spotted next to my left knee. Half crawling and half leaping to where Lammie had rolled, I raised the stone above my head and brought it crashing down into Lammie's face. The descending stone crushed Lammie's nose, crashed into his jaw, sent blood and teeth flying.

I dropped back down to my knees. I continued holding the stone above my head for another strike. But Lammie was dead. I held the stone aloft in triumph, held it in exultation, and let out a shrieking cry of unbounded joy.

My mind was nothing if not elastic. It snapped into lawman mode. I got in the patrol car—*damn I'm glad I'm in the front seat now*—and called, not Marvin, but direct to the dispatcher. "Get the nearest car to my ranch. It's the 283 entrance. Then get Marvin if you can. I've had to shoot a suspect." I didn't mention the stoning. That could come later. I was unconcerned about the legal aspects. I had the situation of being taken here in my own car. I had multiple stab and slashing wounds. The need to kill would not be in dispute. Only I could know that after the derringer did not finish Lammie, I could have arrested him. Without the stone.

A patrol car soon arrived. Marvin drove up a little later, followed shortly by a third car. After all had been done, including protecting the front seat for a fibers test to determine that Lammie had been driving, Marvin had to know. "This the bastard's been stalking you?"

"Yup. It's a long story. Not sure I understand it myself. In fact, I'm sure I don't. Let me talk to you about it in the morning. Tonight I want to spend on the ranch."

Marvin looked at the nicks, the blood all over me. Another deputy had removed my bloody shirt and was applying bandages. "You going to be okay, Cable?"

"I'm wore out. Other than that, okay. Thanks."

One by one the patrol cars left the scene. I headed for the main ranch house, the old home place. I looked forward to seeing Dooley Charter. I looked forward to rest.

Chapter Eleven

To make this story hang together, I have set down some things that Dooley told me.

According to Dooley, my grandfather Cameron Bannerman made a ritual out of looking at his calendar as each day began. He knew he shouldn't enjoy the passing of days, making him older little by little. Somehow he did anyway. As he was about to drink his glass of fruit juice in early morning, he checked the date on the wall calendar hanging near his breakfast table. He already knew the date. He just wanted to see it in print.

He looked forward especially to the first of the month. Today was the first, first of September, 1959. Ceremoniously he lifted a large page of the feed mill calendar and hooked it to the nail holding the calendar, simultaneously hiding August away forever and revealing the new month, hiding the print of a handsome roan at pasture and revealing the print of a grazing buffalo.

He drank the cold juice.

In a few days, the work all done, his wetbacks would be paid off and would leave for the Rio del Norte and their home places in Mexico on the other side.

Cameron smiled a wry grin; "his" wetbacks, indeed. The ones who worked on his place never did return for a successive year. He had talked to fellow ranchers about it. About half of theirs always came back, sometimes more. Some would come back year after year. Banner treated them well. He paid the same wages as other ranchers did, or better. Besides the reassurances his foreman, Jeph Lammie, gave him, he personally observed Jeph's benevolent treatment of them. But they never came back. It had puzzled him at first and it puzzled him now.

He had just finished his pancakes and sausage when Dooley Charter joined him.

"We gotta talk."

"That's a grim look on your face, Dooley. What's aching you?"

"It's grim, all right. I want you to ride with me, let me show you something."

Banner was accustomed to Dooley's mysteries. Without probing for answers, he got up and put on his hat. "Let's go."

Their mounts had been readied for them. With no more conversation, they rode off, Dooley still looking grim and Banner looking bemused. They headed for a remote part of the ranch, Dooley leading the way. Here the terrain rose sharply, and the rock outcroppings would be about as filling for a cow as the sparse grass that sprang here and there from practically no topsoil. The vast Edwards Aquifer gurgled beneath them, far beneath them, and could be tapped with wells, but, unaided by man, there was no water to be had, no seeps and springs, and man had given no aid in these parts. Consequently you saw no cattle here except the occasional stray, and even the far-roaming riders of the Bannerman Ranch seldom came here.

Miles from the headquarters house now, Dooley slowing the pace, Banner spied the cave.

As a boy, he had known the delights of exploring its inner reaches. It didn't reach all that far, so the novelty soon expired. Since then, he couldn't remember even seeing its mouth, the cave being so distant and there being seldom any reason to ride this way.

They drew up and dismounted. He didn't see its mouth now. There were stones that blocked it off. They had weathered together some, but a clue in their unnatural order gave away the artifice of the stone gatherer. Besides, Banner remembered from boyhood that the stones had not been there.

"You've been wondering about your wetbacks, and why you never see 'em again. It has took me awhile, but I've found 'em."

"What you mean, you've found 'em? You been to Mexico?"

Dooley looked down to the ground, then looked to the far horizon in the south. "I got an inkling last year. Then I started asking around. It's funny how fellows who haven't seen anything, don't really know anything, can tell you something anyway. Little pieces. A piece here, a piece there. You might say I was able to get me a theory.

"Then this year, turns out one of the Messicans in the new bunch was related to one of the old ones, one of those who didn't come back here."

Dooley let out his breath and looked back at Banner. "He didn't come back to Mexico either."

Banner tried to fight off the way his thoughts began going.

"What'd the boy tell you?"

"What little he knew. Course he didn't see anything. There were others, like his uncle, didn't come back to Mexico. Managed through the winter, then switched to another ranch. But they'd always send money back to the family. His uncle didn't."

Dooley spat.

"Look, Banner, I didn't want believe this of Jeph Lammie."

"Jeph?" This is what Banner's mind had tried to dodge. "Jeph is probably the best foreman I've had. Never has mistreated the wetbacks."

"Not during the season." Dooley pressed on. "You'd always hand over to Jeph, you know, the payoff, the silver dollars."

"I paid 'em well, considering. They like to get those heavy coins."

"Never did get 'em, Banner. Jeph would bring the crowd up here. It's to the south, on the way to the Rio. Not the usual way, but what's a wetback to complain? He'd line 'em up, then fire off his Winchester. Blam, blam, blam."

Banner looked sick.

Dooley took a step or two towards the cave. "All that was left then was for Jeph to drag the bodies in here."

"He kept the silver."

"Yeah, you never saw it again, just like you didn't ever see your wetbacks again."

"How long did he keep doing this?"

"Since his first year with you. That's four seasons. Lotta silver."

"Lotta wetbacks."

"Wanna look in the cave?"

"No, I don't want to. But I got to."

Dooley, who had rolled away a couple of stones when he inspected the place the day before, rolled away a couple more. Banner went first, crawling up the mound. Dooley pointed a flash over Banner's shoulder. It pinpointed one skeleton at a time. The whole grisly spectacle got put together in his mind.

They backed off the barrow.

Banner brushed himself off. His sick feeling had hardened into disgust. Disgust hardened into anger. Dooley saw a granite face on the old man and saw eyes blazing.

"There's room for one more in that cave. Let's go get the sonofabitch."

Even after they had made the ride back to headquarters, Banner's fury was still at high intensity. His cool judgment had supervened, however, on the fine point of how justice would be meted out to Jeph Lammie. Bannerman had never shrunk from a showdown. But he was an older man now, and besides, he had developed a habit of getting things done for him. His decision was shaped, too, by his sense of irony: The young nephew of one of those skeletons up in the cave would make an end of his uncle's murderer.

Dismounting, he called Doolie over, telling him to fetch the executioner. Lammie had made a day's trip into Gilgal for supplies and would not be around where his suspicions might be aroused.

Bannerman had no concern over being found out, even if he was, which was unlikely, or being troubled about it by anybody. In those days ranchers still handled their own affairs pretty much, without interference from lawmen. Short of performing a wedding, the rancher was like the captain of a seagoing vessel; everything on the ranch was his say-so.

Manuel Elizondo stood in the doorway with Dooley. Bannerman beckoned them on in.

"I sympathize with you in the loss of your uncle. I apologize it happened on my place. It was none of my doing. I guess Dooley has told you that."

"*Sí.*"

Manuel's brief, nervous reply gave Banner no time to form his next remarks. He felt a need to say something else in condolence, maybe something more that was exculpatory.

"We'll . . . uh, we'll give your *tío*, and the others, a Christian funeral when we get done with the matter at hand."

"*Sí. Gracias.*"

"And you know damn well you and *tus compadres* will get the silver you earned. You'll get an extra share to take back to your uncle's widow. Now that's not pay for this job you're going to do. That wouldn't be right, to give pay or take pay for something like that. You understand?"

"*Sí.*"

Manuel understood English well. He spoke it enough to be understood. Banner was fluent in Manuel's language but had made it long practice not to speak it unless absolutely necessary. It bothered him that Manuel would not enter into the conversation more responsively.

"Your uncle earned the silver himself, had it stole by the sorry, murdering bastard that killed him."

"*Sí.*"

"It'll be dark about nine o'clock. Come here to the house. I'll meet you at the side door and give you one of the Springfields. You go to Lammie's cabin. Don't go up to the door. Stand back about six feet. Take a rock in your hand when you head that way. Throw the rock at the door. Lammie will come to the door, probably open up. He doesn't like anybody messing around his place, so he'll come to see. Fire when you see him. Fire twice or more if you have to. Make sure he's dead."

"What about *Senora* Lammie?" Manuel spoke in English.

"I know. You're concerned she'll be a witness. Don't be. I'll settle with her. She'll be glad to be rid of him is my guess. I'll give her money for a new start, her and her baby. You and the *compadres* will hit out for Mexico at daybreak. Besides the silver, I'll give horses to you and them. You can put it all behind you. One more thing. Don't ever come back."

"*Si.*"

"That's for your good, Manuel. That way, no talk, no chance of anybody trying to stir it up, or arrest you."

Manuel's face showed comprehension. He said nothing.

"And, Manuel, you go back to Mexico with a clear conscience. You're not doing murder. This is justice. I have found Lammie guilty, just as much as there had been a judge and jury. You're the executioner."

"*Si*. And *gracias*, *Senor* Banner. You . . . you're a good man."

The business was done. Dooley took Manuel at the elbow and led him out.

It was the night of the new moon. Quiet in his moccasins and rock in hand, Manuel stood in darkness away from the cabin door.

At the crack of the rock against the door, silence fell inside the cabin. There was no outcry. Jeph Lammie opened the door and stood there silhouetted in the yellow glow of a coal oil lamp. He stood there only a moment.

Manuel fired once. The big 1903 Springfield boomed around the pens, the nearby barn, the cabin, and echoed back from the watching hills.

Lammie was thrown back into the cabin by the force of the bullet. Manuel had not moved. In the flickering light he knew, even from that distance, that he saw death. He did not fire again.

Then he silently moved to the door jamb, peering around the corner of the jamb with caution. Now up close, he still saw death.

And death. Unaccountably, the blood-splotched body of *Senora* Lammie lay on the cabin floor behind Lammie's corpse, so close they were touching.

Then life. He saw life. Awakened by the Springfield's boom, a two-year old boy in a makeshift crib was crying gently.

Her and her baby Manuel now remembered hearing *Senor* Banner say. But it hadn't registered with him. He was leaving a mother dead and unexpectedly a surviving child.

Manuel returned the rifle to the side porch of the big house and then went to the quarters. There the *compadres* had heard the great boom of the Springfield. They would have to know. And at daybreak, with new respect for the young Manuel, they would ride for Mexico with silver and with horses. They would remind each other of the cave. It was their good fortune that none of them would see the cave.

Chapter Twelve

WHEN I got to the ranch house, I found that Dooley had nodded off to sleep on the sofa in the Texas room. My entry awoke him and Dooley was stretching as I joined him and took a seat on the sofa.

"Dooley, who the hell was Horace Lammie?"

Dooley would be unprepared for the question wide awake, but drowsy, it was like a punch in the chest. "Never heard of 'im." He could say that honestly, but the Lammie ghost was up and walking.

"He had something to do with the ranch. Said he did. Said his brother came here thirty years ago and never left. Never left alive."

Although Dooley had already determined he would tell me the old story, he had planned to do it his own way at his own time.

"Where'd you talk to him?"

"In my car. On the way to the ranch."

"He's here now?"

"That he is. Like his brother, he'll never leave the ranch, either. In a manner of speaking."

"Whoa, Cable! You got some fillin' in to do."

After I told him of the night's events, Dooley let out a shrill whistle between his teeth. "Well I'll be goddamned."

"What is there to it, Dooley?"

"You're wore out. Get a little sleep. At first light, I'll take and show you something. That's the best way."

I did not want to be put off. But I choked down the demand that was forming in my craw. Dooley was right. I was wore out.

It would be a few miles' ride, so Dooley and I sat down to scrambled eggs, sausage, and biscuits before setting out.

"Yeah, Horace Lammie's brother was here, back in the 50s. Name was Jeph. Jephunneh Lammie. He was foreman. Like Horace said, Jeph never left the ranch. I never had heard of Horace 'til you called his name last night. Didn't know Jeph had a brother."

"What became of this Jeph?"

"Your granddaddy had trouble with him."

"So he was killed."

"He got what he deserved."

I thought this over. Last week Dooley had finally agreed, sort of, to reveal something that would help me resolve my quandary over why I enjoyed the prospect of law enforcement violence so much. So this was it. My grandfather had been the same way. A good man, but killed when he had to. And enjoyed it. Jeph Lammie was probably not the first, maybe not the last.

"See, Lammie had killed some hands. I'm gonna show you this. So your granddaddy had him shot."

Had him shot? What is this? How does this square with the hot-blooded lineage I thought I was beginning to discover? "You mean Banner hired a hit man?"

"Not a hit man. Wasn't like that. Anyway, his bones has been here on the ranch these thirty years. That's why his brother come lookin' for you. But I can't figger how he ever got on to it. Now he's dead on the ranch, too."

"What I meant was, he'll never leave alive. I had his body taken in to Gilgal. But he was killed on the ranch. Thirty years ago my granddaddy killed one brother, and last night I killed the other one. What do you think of that, Dooley?"

What Dooley was thinking, Dooley wasn't saying. We had finished our plates. One last swig of java, and Dooley was on his feet.

"Let's saddle up."

When we got in sight of the cave, I felt only a slight familiarity with the surrounding hills and arroyos. Because the barrow was set against the mouth of the cave, I had never known it was a cave and was not drawn here as a boy would be.

In a coulee still some distance from the cave, we dismounted and began to walk the rest.

Dooley said, "Banner was puzzled when the Messicans never came back from year to year. Then when he found out that Jeph Lammie was killing 'em for the sake of silver, he went into a quiet rage like I had never seen before. He dealt with it before even one more sun rose."

I made no reply. Words didn't come to me out of the horror that Dooley disclosed.

We were at the cave. Rolling several rocks from

the weathered barrow, Dooley let in a little light. Each with a flash in hand, Dooley and I, atop what was now left of the mound, could see most of the bones.

This is what Dooley wanted me to see. Dooley was more comfortable with artifacts than words. Before the provocation of Horace Lammie's surprise arrival, Dooley's intention had been to show me the cave and the bones and then fill in the story of how they came to be there. He had never known, had never been able to settle in his own mind, how much he would reveal to me.

"We gave 'em a Christian ceremony, just as Banner had promised Manuel. We did that the next day. Lammie's wife, her name was Mahlah, she was called Molly, had been killed accidentally, we found out, by the same bullet that struck Lammie. Went through him, still had enough force to kill her. Banner put her body in the cave, a little apart from the rest, and she got the same ceremony the Messicans did, Banner saying she was a victim of Lammie just like they were. Then he put Lammie in, over to the side there, and said as little as he could over him. Later I got rid of the Springfield. Banner didn't want it around anymore because it would be a reminder."

I had never heard Dooley say so much at a stretch. I listened for more. I knew there had to be more.

"Her little two-year old boy had to be cared for. That night I rigged him a little bunk in my room."

Dooley abruptly quit talking. Was there not going to be anymore?

Maybe it was the bones. Dooley looked at them for only the third time, the first time almost thirty years ago. The sight stunned him once more, breaking the seal of silence he had maintained so long.

It was like plowing. Once in the furrow, Dooley would not stop. But even plowing, you had to get your breath. Dooley wished he was plowing.

With effort he rolled away one more stone from the diminished barrow. It was a large stone. Then he had to meet my eyes up close. He put his hand on the my shoulder.

"That little baby boy, that was you, Cable."

I completely lost any composure I had. I lost more than that. The ensuing moments were surreal. The grackles had been screaming their piercing screams all during Dooley's monologue but I had not heard them. Now it was as if their powerful shrieks were aimed with delight at me. The large, purplish black birds, I thought, were swooping toward me, now one, now two, now more, attending to my discomfort. "It means . . ." they seemed to shriek. "It means . . ."

"No, it can't mean that!" I cried to the sky. Unwillingly I myself took up the grackles' chorus. "It means . . . it means . . ."

Dooley was aghast at what he was witnessing.

I had slowly wandered, my knees buckling with each step. My arms were half-outstretched, because I could manage no more, outstretched towards . . . the sky? . . . the swooping grackles?

Dooley thought he should move closer to me, move to support me, to touch me. Instead he watched as I finally slipped to the parched ground on my knees, my fists beating a tattoo on the stones. Why had I stumbled closer to the crypt? I wanted to get away, not get closer. I wished I'd never seen it, never heard of it.

The grackles were now distant, barely audible, drawn by whim or purpose as birds may be drawn, to another place. Now the low winds could again be heard, through the arroyos and around the Texas hills.

I had subsided. My sanity was returning in bits and pieces. *Is that what sanity is? Is it bits and pieces, and if a man is lucky he can pull them together with his will, when he needs to, and when he can?*

Reaching for Dooley but not quite making it, I said, "It means . . ."

Now I knew what it meant. I had wanted to know, and now I knew. "Dooley," I began softly. "You've stood by me. You've led me to see what I wanted to know. What I thought I wanted to know. There's no blame on you, Dooley."

I choked and could say no more. Dooley had talked long and was talked out. We went back in silence to the coulee for our horses.

Dooley wished he'd never have to talk again, but back at the ranch house he had to make the explanation that knitted everything together, or ripped it apart, depending on how you looked at it. In his own words and in his own way, Dooley told me what old Banner had done after the deaths of Jeph and Molly Lammie.

"The baby has to be looked after," Banner told Dooley. "I hadn't calculated this. I expected the mother not to be killed but to leave the ranch with the child."

Banner didn't even know the little boy's name. Molly could read, which meant she could read the Bible, the only book she'd ever seen. She could write a little, not in a plain hand, but enough to make entries in the family Book. Banner took the volume, modest in size and material, from the little cabin. At his desk he observed that it was not a King James Version. *Molly had had little money,* he reflected, *but you pay little and still get the richness of the King James. And it's copyrighted,* he noted to himself, absently, *like all Bibles. Odd thing.*

There in the front were the pages, still mostly blank, where Molly had made the sparse entries that stood for her brief life. Banner copied down my name, Cable, and the date of my birth. Later, when the plan already formed in his mind was in place, he would write my name and date in a larger, more expensive Bible, the same one in which I, when grown, would find it my duty to write.

He opened the Lammie family's Bible to where he saw a narrow purple ribbon serving as a bookmark. It was at Numbers 14. In verse 18, a portion of one line was marked: "The Lord . . . visits the iniquity of the fathers upon the children unto the third and fourth generations." Then, twelve verses later: "Caleb the son of Jephunneh."

Then Banner burned Molly's little Bible. He had never had to dispose of a Bible before, but he knew you could burn a tattered old flag, with respect, and he figured you could burn a Bible that way. What Molly took to her grave was a secret, the mistake of it not even known to her when she lived. Struggling to make the entry as fitting as she could for its importance, even for its sacredness, Molly transposed one letter. Banner could not learn from her tiny written legacy that Molly called her child Caleb, the name she had given me at birth.

Banner's wife had died in the year. His only son, Chisholm, didn't get along with Banner all that well and didn't really like ranch life. Maybe the two went together. He and his wife Lucy had left the ranch, that was about three years before, and were living in the state of Washington. They had had no children.

Banner placed a long distance call. "Chisholm, how about coming back to the ranch? You ever think about it?"

"You called at a good time. I have been thinking about it. This business I'm trying to run is not doing all that well."

"How about Lavinnia? You think she'd be interested?"

"Lucy, Papa. You know she doesn't like to be called Lavinnia."

"Okay. Lucy. Listen, tell Lucy there's a two-year-old boy here needs a mama."

"Where'd a two-year-old boy come from?"

"I'll explain it all later. He's Anglo, in good health."

"Truth is, that would clinch it for Lucy. She . . . we . . . want a child, haven't been able to have one. Let me ask her."

When Chisholm got back on the line, it was evident Banner's entreaties had fallen on receptive ears. In a month, Chisholm and Lucy were back on the ranch. I, their little son Cable Bannerman, had bright prospects.

In time, anybody who knew anything about it, except Banner and Dooley, and of course the new mama and daddy, was gone. Personal and family friends were under the impression the young couple had brought their baby back from the west coast with them.

Lucy found that besides being healthy, I was cheerful and alert. Banner recalled that he had often seen Molly with her baby boy outside the cabin, showing me the ranch animals, talking with me, making toys out of simple things that came to hand. I had had a good mother. Now I had a second one, a green-eyed brunette mother, looking a little bit like Ava Gardner, who loved me as if I were her own.

Chisholm worked hard. He had always done that. But what he did and the way he did it didn't always suit Banner. About a year had passed when he joined his papa in the Texas room one night after supper.

"I thought it would work. I've tried to make it work. Maybe I'm not cut out for it. I've found a business I can buy in West Virginia, similar to the one I had on the West Coast."

"Chisholm, you know I wish you'd stay here, you and Lucy. But I didn't stop you before, and I'm not stopping you now. I'll help you get started there. I'll do as much as you want me to."

Lucy joined them. "We want to take Cable. Not now, I don't mean that. I mean after we get settled there."

"He's your little boy, Lucy, yours and Chisholm's. Of course he's going to live with you. But I'll miss him. Promise me there'll be a lot of ranch visits."

"I promise, Papa."

A week later Chisholm and Lucy set out for the east. Three days after they drove away, Banner got the telephone call telling him they had been killed in a car crash on icy roads near Huntington.

So there was Banner and there was Dooley. Two fellows kept the boy; two fellows kept the secret.

I raced to Gilgal in my patrol car.

From Dooley I had learned one more thing—that Benjamin Edes had earlier learned my family secret and then had become the urging influence that caused Dooley to disclose it to me. Still shaken to my roots by what I had learned and seen at the cave, I began to seethe, then to rage, in my mind. I was raging at Ben Edes. I had trusted Ben. I had looked up to Ben. Ben had betrayed me, I decided.

Such was my outward composure as I entered Ben's office that Ben saw no change in me.

We exchanged howdies and I said, "Here it is Friday, Ben, you don't have to get a paper out again 'til Monday. Come on out to the ranch with me. I want to show you something."

Always ready to go on a lark, Ben agreed.

In the patrol car as we made our way west, Ben easily fell into the topic that had absorbed us both for so long now, our favorite and usual conversation. I did not make frequent objections and sallies as I ordinarily did. When you're a talker, it's hard to fault a good listener, but the truth is that what I was doing was mean spirited. I had discovered my horrible truth, the truth Ben had tried to help me seek. I had no further use for Ben's tutelage. I had come to despise it. I was letting Ben go on just to get more of the same on recent record.

One of my few interjections came when Ben made one of his sweeping statements about the value of liberal arts.

"Hell, Ben, you liberal arts folks make promises all the time you can't keep. You've never paid heed to Chuck Butterworth's song, 'Don't Let Your Lips Make Promises Your Body Can't Keep.' One of these college deans heard a rich alumnus make a speech praising liberal arts. The dean started telling students their degrees would get jobs for them in business and industry. Trouble was, the alumnus was a C.E.O., but when the lowly recruiters came to campus, they still looked for somebody who could set up an accounting program or do marketing studies or something. I saw in your own newspaper that sixty or seventy percent of the liberal arts graduates find their degrees of no use in getting jobs, and that's after three or four years of looking after they graduate."

Ben said, "That diatribe is particularly harsh coming from you."

I wasn't finished. "Then you and the professors like to talk about 'what it means to be human' and stuff like that. 'Learn how to live, not just how to make a living.' That's a tub of hogwash. It would do a better job and cost a hell of a lot less to send the kids to Sunday School, make them take an oath to obey the Boy Scout and Girl Scout laws."

"Cable, you're not that simple minded."

"Listen, I happened to see three bishops, or whatever they were, on television boasting about what their little liberal arts colleges had to offer that was special. Course it was values, and living to help your fellow man, and all the usual puffery. By coincidence, those same colleges were featured in an education newspaper the same week. Guess what their admissions counselors were telling prospects to lure them to come pay that high tuition and what was 'special' about the college? That they got on campus the best rock bands! They talk about 'learning to live,' but, by God, it's making a living for them. That's all it is, Ben, profiteering and no truth in advertising."

Ben had grown perplexed. Missing was my usual humor in bantering with my old mentor. Ben fell silent. The rest of the way he commented on wildflowers, new fencing being strung, some cows he saw. I said nothing more.

At the ranch, I took the Jeep, a concession to Ben's aversion to extended stretches on horseback. I waved to Dooley who was over by the windmill doing something to it. Dooley returned the wave.

To Ben's eyes, my mood seemed to have brightened on the ride to the cave, and he put the fractious exchanges out of his mind. When the Jeep pulled to a stop, Ben spied the cave. "Just the adventure for a couple of youngsters like us—a little spelunking."

"Spoken like a liberal arts man who has read about the experience but has never seen the inside of a cave. Real cavers can't stand being called spelunkers."

I took a large prying bar from the Jeep and a gasoline lantern. Using the leverage of the bar, I rolled away the remaining large stones. Now we could enter the ragged cave by hunching down and, once inside, stand erect. I fired off the lantern before entering. In the bright, steady glow from the mantel, Ben saw the bones. And more bones. Gradually, the whole grisly heap of remains.

In years of reporting, he had seen enough of everything from fresh corpses to disinterred skeletons to recognize, as he already had reason to know, he was being shown something a decade or more dead. Ben did not tip his hand. "You're not giving me a lead on a breaking story, are you." It was not a question.

"Could be. Who says when a case is closed?"

In an even voice, I related the story I had just this morning learned, the story Ben had already heard from Dooley. The sorrow in Ben's face changed into a grief-like sympathy.

"So there's your higher learning, Ben.

Sociobiology, you said. It's in your genes, you said. Learn more about it, you said, and then you'll understand it."

They were facing each other in the lantern's bright glow.

"So now I understand I come from a long line of murdering bastards. This finishes me."

"And you blame me for it? It wasn't books that led you here. That trail went cold. It was Dooley led you here, at your insistence." Ben was standing pat.

"Leave Dooley out of this. You're the one who urged me on. You sang the siren song of higher learning. I'm done, Benjamin, and so are you."

I drew the revolver from my holster. I raised it level with the eyes of Benjamin Edes.

Ben saw that it was an old model, older even than the skeletons that kept us company. He was not going to plead for his life. He had more pride than that. He would reason with his protégé.

"It's far from being too late for you or too late for me. There are ways to understand this, ways to deal with it. There are things I can tell you."

I tightened my grip on the old revolver. I drew the hammer back.

"Start talking."

Chapter Thirteen

"Maybe if I say something good about A & M you won't shoot me."

"Not funny."

"I want to. Then I can say nobody ever said anything good about A & M unless an Aggie held a gun on him."

My gun remained aimed at the bridge of Ben's nose and it stayed cocked. I felt myself relaxing a little.

Ben was encouraged. "I predict that A & M in time will be recognized as the best undergraduate university in the state of Texas."

If the cave could hear, even the cave would have thought this prosaically worded statement to be odd to the circumstances. Even in my tortured state of mind I thought so, at some almost out-of-touch level of consciousness. Now the cast of my face must have shown a further relaxation. Did my revolver waver just a hair?

"Cable, you were raised a Bannerman. You're still a Bannerman. I know I've been strongly influenced by the sociobiologists, but I've never said environment is of no consequence. Think about your modernist murder suspect. He killed because he is so convinced your habitat shapes you, even saves you. We're in your habitat right now. Just a couple of miles away is the big, comfortable ranch house where you became a Bannerman."

I was still in no mood to be convinced of anything expressed in mere talk, especially right now, Ben's talk. Yet my erratic surge of anger that had brought us to this killing place had subsided some in the passage of time. And my memories of boyhood provoked by Ben's mention of the ranch house were flooding in like a cooling, refreshing rain.

My move was sudden, instantaneous. Like a curtain dropping on a stage production that has played to its end, I released the hammer harmlessly and dropped the revolver from Ben's face to its place in my holster. Then all six-feet-plus of me sagged. "Ben . . ." I began.

Although confident, in one part of his mind, that the crisis had passed, Ben felt a powerful urge to get the hell out of the threatening cave. He reached for the bail of the lantern, keeping his eyes on me. Picking it up, he headed out of the place. I followed as if I were trailing the lamp of knowledge.

"Our little drama has ended," Ben said when we emerged into the already fading late afternoon sunlight. "The crisis has passed."

He handed the gasoline lantern to me. I extinguished the flame.

"You know what a crisis is, Cable, for I have told you. Widespread ignorance has robbed the word of its unique usefulness, making it a synonym for misfortune. It means, as you will recall, a turning point. The result may be horrible, but it may be wonderful."

Now I could not help but smile, thinking of the incongruity of the form Ben's mini-lecture took. Ben the born teacher would teach at the drop of a hat, or in this case at the drop of revolver back into its holster.

Back in the cave I had relented. Now I became remorseful. "Something just took me over, Ben. What I found out about myself this morning was more than I could handle. Now I've found out something else, that I would turn on you like that."

"It's called 'killing the messenger,' Cable. Happens all the time. Newspaper people are accustomed to it."

"Yeah, 'killing the messenger.' That sure fits. I can see something else. You lash out at the nearest person, and more likely than not the nearest person is the one that has stood by you."

We shook hands, got in the Jeep, and headed back to ranch headquarters.

Inside, Dooley poured a round of sour mash, neat. He asked no questions. Then I drove Ben back to Gilgal.

I knew I had to be with Linda Faye. Stopping at my apartment only long enough to telephone her, clean up, and change into civvies, I went to her place already lighter in spirit.

During Gideon Lincecum's preparation for the Alexander Meredith murder trial, I unexpectedly got to know Meredith better. I had turned over case prep to the district attorney. The D.A. and his staff members were back and forth through my office to the big room all the time, and I was assisting them when called upon. Meredith had been denied bond. He persuaded a jailer to deliver a message to me.

"He wants you to come to his cell and talk to him."

I pondered the request. It did not violate the law, I concluded, and accompanied the jailer down one flight of stairs to the basement jail.

Inside Meredith's cubicle, I saw a prisoner whose demeanor was little changed. Even his 'stripe-ed britches' seemed to take on a fashion note suitable to their wearer.

"I guess I'm obliged to remind you that anything you say can still be held against you."

"Everything material that I tell you, I have told or will tell my attorney. I want him fully informed when he strides forth to defend me. What I seek in this meeting with you is your understanding. Your testimony will not be affected one whit by what I disclose to you."

"It's your call."

"I executed Phil G. Swinton, Sheriff Bannerman. He deserved to die. I did not think much of the consequences, although I concede that I did not anticipate your ingenuity in identifying me. I thought I would be scot-free.

"Why was my unusual motive strong enough to compel me to commit the act? In my long career I have accomplished quite enough to benefit my fellow man, but in retirement my work languished. I wanted to serve again, and to serve by disposing of Swinton. Being a superior person I am convinced of my right to do so."

Meredith smiled wickedly. "Truth be told, I became intrigued by the intricacies of the plot. Who knows, who can ever know, the motivations that dovetail as one plans a . . . a *frappé du morte*, let alone that in this instance society calls it a crime. Maybe in the end I was as much propelled by the prospect of access through the little panel, obtaining and later disposing of the weapon, lettering the card in honor of my old friend Gropius . . ."

Meredith trailed off, a distant look on his face. ". . . as much propelled by fascination with those things as with the grander purpose I first had in mind."

"Like I said, it's your call, but this all goes to motive. It becomes testimony to your state of mind and clearly admissible."

"Tut tut. My motive will be my defense, Sheriff Bannerman. Look here, I seek your understanding, not to affect my trial, but merely for my own satisfaction. And I seek it on the grounds—you understand the grapevine has been active, even into the precincts of this ill-designed place of incarceration—on the grounds your grandfather took the law into his own hands, likewise, and rid the world of an undesirable cretin."

I was stung by the revelation that word had gotten around but pleased that the architect still referred to Banner as my grandfather.

"You yet take pride in him, do you not, in spite of learning one of his noblest acts was against your natural father? In looking into me, you have had to look into Bauhaus, I know. You will therefore not be surprised to hear me declare you still, and forevermore, a Bannerman!"

I uttered no word of assent but was surprised to hear myself beginning to tell of my escape from Horace Lammie. I had come to the cell to listen, not to talk. I left out the part about the stone I had brought down on my uncle's head.

Meredith, however, had already heard how Horace Lammie had met his death. Besides, he was too acute to trifle with in matters of intonation and subtlety. He read my wish to destroy. "Strong men, men of justice, give them their leeway! Your grandfather would understand. You and I understand."

You and I. I had been coupled with the avenging modernist. I felt, indeed, that Meredith's words had riveted us together. I regretted I had said anything.

"Will you tell me that you understand?"

"I'll tell you that I admire your unflinching courage as you face trial." Lawman training had taken back over; I was being circumspect.

But what I had already said was enough. A look of satisfaction spread over Meredith's face. "We'll meet again, Sheriff Bannerman. It won't be here. I assure you I will trouble you no more to come visit me in my present abode. Of course there will be the trial, but I mean after that, we'll meet again."

It did not seem to comport with jail cell propriety, but I shook Meredith's hand. Other than that, I was all business, if wry. "Thanks for inviting me to drop in on you."

I returned slowly up the stairs, but my mind was racing. I could not condone murder, as much as I had despised Swinton and as much as I had come to think of Meredith. You could not take the law into your own hands. What I myself did was different; I *was* the law. It's true I did believe in individual liberty. I thought government in the United States had grown far too large. I was opposed to the welfare state and had been heard to denounce Lyndon

Johnson's Great Society as an abomination. But there had to be law. There had to be at least a little more than law, some protection for the meek before they went through Heaven's probate.

I longed to reach the top of the stairs, to return to my own office where the law was the law, and where I would be reassured by seeing the plaque on the wall. Oh, the plaque. Ben was wrong about my not being introduced to the higher learning at A & M.

I had gone for awhile with a gorgeous woman who was a philosophy major. That's how I had been introduced to the higher learning. More could be said. To the present point, it is enough to reflect that she had become fascinated with Schiller. It was the philosophy in his histories, poems, and plays that drew her. As is true of many enthusiasms of the sophomore year, it was not lasting. One of Schiller's lines became enduring for me, however. The young Aggie woman had quoted it to me. When I showed high interest in it, she had it engraved on a plaque and gave it to me for my birthday. I stepped into my office now and read it still again:

"Nür das Gesetz ist die Freiheit geben."
Only within order is freedom possible.

Chapter Fourteen

ALEXANDER Meredith could not have found an advocate who suited him better than Gideon Lincecum. He might have found one who would have served him better. Lincecum did not, as an attorney bent on saving his client from the death penalty might, try to dissuade Meredith from making the bizarre defense of justifiable homicide. Rather, Lincecum delighted in it.

I testified as a sheriff should, doing the defendant no favors.

Meredith took the stand in his own behalf, of course. Lincecum drew so much from him on direct that little was left to the prosecutor except to attempt to expose the architect's egoism to ridicule.

In the closing, the defense attorney gave up nothing in grandeur to his flamboyant client. Thrilling the packed courtroom with flourishes seldom heard in Gilgal, or anywhere anymore, he was addressing a spellbound jury by the time he reached his dramatic conclusion.

"Andrew Hamilton, defending John Peter Zenger in that legendary landmark case that established freedom of the press in this country, faced a law that would not allow truth as a defense against a charge of libel. But that *was* his client's defense. My client's defense is his right to put to death an evil man, Phil G. Swinton.

"The prosecutor contends the law does not allow it? I say to you, as Andrew Hamilton said to that jury long ago, 'If it is not the law, it *should* be the law!'"

One juror was observed beaming with satisfaction, as if in victory.

The panel stayed out and stayed out. After three days, the initial division of eleven to one for conviction had been whittled to seven to five. The dissenter, alone at first, had convinced four they should vote with him. He could do no more, but the jury was hung.

Through Pepys Fowler, I later learned the holdout was a closet objectivist, devotee of Ayn Rand and, like Meredith, owner of a copy of *Night of January 16th*. As lethal as the little play could prove, the juror owned something Meredith did not. No one could say whether he read the play over and over, but Pepys confirmed that the juror cleaned and oiled his AK-47 weekly.

I made no disclosure of Pepys's findings to the district attorney. As the latter pondered his decision whether to re-try the defendant, he had only the knowledge of the seven-to-five jury split. Meredith was freed on bond. There was no public outrage as gradually life got back to normal for everyone involved in the case, save Phil G. Swinton.

"Linda Faye, life sure has gotten dull around here, except when I'm with you, sweetie."

"I don't know how you stand it, buck-o. No big murder to solve, no election to win, nobody stalking you. But that's what you said you wanted, a leisurely second term."

I put a bookmark in the Texas history I had looked up from when I spoke to Linda Faye, closed it, and put it down. We were spending the weekend at the ranch.

"My own search is over, so I don't crave the leisure."

"Your search will never be over, Cable. You're the searchingest fellow I've ever known. You're just searching for something different now."

"How'd you know?"

Linda Faye, who had been looking out into a meadow, turned slowly to face me. What she saw in my expression she had never seen before, and couldn't figure what to make of it.

"How'd I know *what?*"

I put my arm around her. "Here in my pocket I've got..."

"Don't start telling me what's in your damn pocket," she laughed.

"Linda Faye, listen to me. You know a fellow is at his most tongue-tied when he..."

"Cable?"

"When he... well, Linda Faye..."

I took a little jeweler's box from one of my trouser pockets. Opening it, and not with the steady hands for which I was known, I held a diamond engagement ring before her. "... when he asks a woman to be his bride."

Her answer was a soft squeal. "Oh-h-h!"

I slid the ring onto Linda Faye's finger. We both reflected later that I had never asked her and she had never said yes. Just "When a fellow . . ." and "Oh-h-h!"

You would think Linda Faye and I would have been the most excited people in Gilgal and Joshua County. It wasn't for lack of our own delight, but when a divorcee who is thirty-eight gets engaged, that's something, and when an eligible young bachelor sheriff and rancher is caught, that's something, so the double bill was almost more than the folks could adequately enjoy.

The ceremony took place on the ranch in the great hall. The reception started in the Texas room but then meandered outside, on the side porch, the front porch, under arbors, and around the barbecue pit. Pepys Fowler and Dooley Charter got together on the arrangements. Fanny Wright had finished her internship, which was the final requirement for her degree in law enforcement, but she didn't have a job yet. She came up a week ahead to help out. Marvin was no more help than I was.

After a late afternoon wedding, the reception went on into the night, Linda Faye and I staying until the last. The last was the five-piece western swing band playing "Maiden's Prayer." Then we headed to Galveston for a long honeymoon.

The year continued idyllic.

Linda Faye was concerned, when she told me she was going to have a baby, that it might reawaken my old desperate thoughts concerning the provenance of my bloodline. Quite the contrary. I was no longer obsessed with an urge to slay miscreants. Whether I was mostly influenced by the reading Ben had had me do, or the dreadful confrontation with old bones and an old truth, I did not know. Maybe it owed to my face-off with Ben, or a combination of these things. Besides, the fantasy that captures most of us captured me. To say a baby is coming means it's coming from who knows where, that at its appointed time it will suddenly appear. To know that it was growing inside the woman who slept touching me at night was no match for the power of make-believe. It followed, then, that the baby, the young boy or girl, would be its own person unfettered by tags of pedigree.

Then when the baby boy did miraculously appear, these convictions strengthened in me. I would listen with amusement as the inevitable likenesses were discovered, as many likenesses as there were enchanted viewers. I, on the other hand, saw a unique creature. Linda Faye and I named the child Matt. That syllable was quite long enough for the little fellow, and for years the name Matthew George Bannerman would appear quietly only in the old Bannerman family Bible and on his birth certificate.

Family lines do not stretch out unalloyed forever, I reflected. In fact they cannot survive one generation without admixture. The birth of little Matt bolstered my self regard. I had made peace with my natural origin, now assumed to be Lammie, not Bannerman. Briefly I entertained the fantasy that Banner, my assumed grandfather, was in fact my sire. He could have enjoyed a peccadillo with Mollie, my real mother. So I would be a Bannerman after all. But for more than one reason I gave up on the notion. I began to think more of my mother. I came to the sensible conclusion that the maternal line is the only one of which anyone can be absolutely certain, no matter how well-born. You could say that I was of sound mind—and "green broke!"

That Linda Faye was Matt's mother clinched it all, anyway.

When I got to my office one morning, I soon received the first of the telephone calls complaining about a new environmental measure. There were so many I finally cut them off. I had not gotten around to reading the previous day's issue of *Harry's of the West*. I picked it up and found the article that was causing the torrent of calls. I began to read it. Readers had taken it to be the truth. Could it be true?

"Thirty-three counties in the Texas Hill Country have been placed under a sweeping order designed to protect the winter habitat of the rosy-eyed snowbird. The creature is native to Michigan, Minnesota, and that general vicinity.

"Attractions which draw the snowbird to the fabled area would be restricted. No historic structures could be razed without federal approval. A spokesman for the agency explained that protected structures included ranch houses, abandoned filling stations, barns, and privies.

"'Even fence posts are covered under this order,' the rulemaker explained. 'Rosy-eyed snowbirds find fence posts to be picturesque and often stop to photograph them. They take close-up pictures of the barbed wire (bobwire).'

"A rancher whose spread lies along both sides of Turtle Creek responded angrily, 'If a man can't tear down his own privy, then property rights don't mean a damn thing anymore!'

"He explained that he was caught between the

rulings of two federal agencies. 'The health people have told me the privy is unsanitary and has to be torn down. The environmental nuts have threatened to slap a big fine on me if I so much as take one board or nail out of it.'

"The inclusion of privies in the unprecedented protective action also has provoked a turf war in Washington. Hillary Clinton considers privies to be in her domain because of her czar-like, if unofficial, authority over health care. Surgeon General Jocelyn Elders heatedly replied she would not give up her authority over privies. 'One-holers, two-holers, whatever, I'm the one in charge of privies, not only in the Texas Hill Country but all across the United States.'

"A leak from the First Lady's staff revealed that she is planning to establish a forty-four-member Privy Commission, which she will sit in on. Washington insiders say the resulting publicity would effectively silence the Surgeon General in the privy area. Historical records show that it would be the first time anyone has been silenced in the privy area.

"Agency officials defended their order. 'We're acting in the spirit of Vice President Gore's government streamlining plan. People won't have to apply individually to get their property on the National Register of Historic Places. Think of the paper work that will be eliminated. Every single ranch, residence, business, and site in the thirty-three counties will be on the Register, whether the owners want them to be or not.'

"One Gilgal citizen, Ara B. Wharton, said bluntly, 'Let the snowbirds go back where they came from.'

"Again we are witness to the cheek of Ara B."

I sighed. Even if the first sentence didn't tip off readers to the satire, the last line should have.

There's only one railroad tunnel in Texas. Everybody knows that. But they're wrong.

Joshua County adjoins Kendall County, and in Kendall is what's left of the old tunnel where once ran the tracks of the Fredericksburg & Northern Railway. Now it's home to bats. It's generally thought to be the only railroad tunnel in Texas.

A few cowboys know about the other one. In far west Texas, long ago, coal was discovered within the confines of a vast box canyon. Seasoned riders could get in and out and presumably had done so for centuries. It was a hidden canyon only in the same sense the Americas were the New World. To most eyes, however, it remains lost.

To mine coal and get it out in commercial quantities was a different matter. That's why they dug the tunnel and laid rails. The cars had long since ceased to run. The tunnel now was a little-known entry to the Coal Mine Ranch.

I got the call late one afternoon. It was Tom Lenard, sheriff of Fillmore County. "You been keeping up with our little ruckus out here?"

"I've been reading the papers. Sounds like you could use the tourist trade."

"Everybody and his brother. The film commission has been promising us a movie. Instead we get a three-ring militia."

"How you going to get 'em out of there?"

"I was about to ask you the same question."

"Me? It's not my county."

"Cable, I want you to come out here and take command of this thing. You've got military experience, I don't. That gives you an edge. I've got my hands full just trying to administer this nuisance, liaison and that sort of stuff."

"Why not bring the feds in?"

"I can't stand 'em around. They wouldn't come anyway. A case of burnt hands after Waco."

"What about the Texas Rangers?"

"Don't ever say I said this, Cable. They're a helluva fine force, and I admire 'em. I just . . . professional jealousy on my part, I guess . . . I'd just rather keep control in my county myself. I need a field commander. You're the one who can do the job, ol' podnuh."

In my mind, I already had my gear packed. I delayed a little more, talked about arrangements and authority, and got satisfied. "I'll take it on, Tom. I'll head that way starting at daybreak tomorrow."

A militia group had holed up in Coal Mine Ranch. In that remote area they posed no threat to the sovereignty of the State of Texas or even to Fillmore County. Trouble is, they were breaking the law. They had dispossessed the owners of Coal Mine Ranch.

The standoff was in its third week, time enough for me to have already devised, just out of curiosity and not because I had any idea I would get the responsibility, a plan for an attack that would end the militia's pretensions. In my imagination, they would all be killed.

That's the way my mind still works, I reflected.

I was pretty sure that no one, except Linda Faye, had noticed any outward change in me since I saw the cave and heard the grackles. I myself, on the other hand, had the feeling of being inside a vacuum. I tried to think of myself as a Bannerman, and mostly it worked. Yet, my rationale for dispensing frontier justice had been eroded some. *Jeph Lammie, a sorry, greedy murderer, that's who was really my sire.* I would chase the thought out of my mind every time it slipped to the fore.

The way I was beginning to win the struggle was by concentrating on only my first name. *I am Cable. What I am, I am. What I have done, I have done.* I worked my thoughts around to where I made the vacuum an advantage, or a convenience. I could feel myself physically floating free in the vacuum.

I was floating free when I got the summons from Tom Lenard. I wanted to go to Coal Mine Ranch. I would go. I would do what I damn well pleased. Before I could catch myself I thought *I would kill every bastard in there if that's what it took.*

Chapter Fifteen

MY first inclination was to leave Marvin in charge in Joshua County, but there would be routine to be handled at Coal Mine Ranch, just as there was here. I had to take Marvin with me. I called him to the office and laid the whole thing out for him. The first task I assigned Marvin was lining up the rest of the crew I wanted to take.

I myself called in C. A. Rodney, a promising deputy who could benefit from acting as sheriff. "Call me if anything big breaks, C. A., or anything you're not comfortable with. I'll come, or Marvin will." I dashed off a handwritten note and posted it on the bulletin board, announcing C. A.'s appointment.

Marvin had gone to work getting the crew together for the next day's early departure. He enlisted Pepys Fowler and was fortunate to find Fanny Wright, still without a job, visiting Pepys, and signed her on as I wanted. O. B. agreed to go. Ben accepted my request that he handle public relations on the mission.

Marvin took a deep breath before placing the next call. "How," he had asked me, "do you think you can get by with having a felon on your task force?"

"He's not a felon, Marvin; he was not convicted. Anybody who can kill somebody who is locked in from the inside should be able to figure out how to launch an attack into a box canyon. An architect has a knack for three-dimensional things. I want Alexander Meredith with us."

Marvin picked up the telephone and dialed the number. Over the line came Meredith's stately "Ye-es?"

After Marvin put it to him, Meredith replied with one question. "Your place or mine?"

Marvin told him we'd pick him up, please be outside the front door, packed up and ready to board.

Then Marvin went to work on what I wanted for transportation. "Get us a band bus, like Willie Nelson travels in." Marvin didn't blink. Everybody knew Marvin was resourceful. Marvin knew it, too.

"Hey, Sonny," he said over the telephone to the owner of a custom bus outfitter place in Austin, "I know you remember that favor you owe me."

"Never will forget it. You won't let me. I think I've paid you back two or three times already. Whatcha need?"

"A tour bus. Can't be very old, fairly low mileage. Where we're going, it's got to be dependable."

"Well, ol' buddy, you live a charmed life. You must have paid your ten. Gotta pay your ten if you want to get in. I've got a repossession, beautiful bus, brand-new really. A little band had a record deal. Thought they did. Then the Japanese or some damn body bought the company, reneged on the contract."

"I've got to have it tonight, Sonny."

"Well, why didn't you say so. I got the repo papers signed this morning, haven't even gone to bring it back. The boys took delivery on it just last week. I think all they've done is drive it back to their place, show off a little bit."

"Where's their place?"

"You ready for this, Marvin? The bus is settin' over there in Junction in the next county to you."

Marvin whistled. Even he was not supposed to be this resourceful. They made a deal on the lease terms, and Marvin was out the door, calling to another deputy to drive him to Junction and telling me the crew was all lined up and where he was going.

Marvin stayed up all night fetching the bus, gassing up, and stocking the onboard refrigerator and cabinets. At the suggestion of the bandleader, he got the water supply topped off. The leader told him they hadn't peed in the toilet all that much, but all their buddies in Junction had wanted to flush it just to see it work.

One look at sleepy Marvin, and I pulled another deputy onto the crew as driver at the last minute. There was a special passenger I had wanted to bring, Linda Faye, but I couldn't think of any excuse. She didn't want to leave little Matt in someone else's care anyway. She always had good ideas, but I'd just have to get them over the telephone. She had hugged me goodbye with admonitions against acting reckless.

All hands boarded at the court house except Meredith, who was waiting on his front porch when we pulled up. Besides his grip he was carrying a satchel containing survey instruments. I assigned seats. My military mind prompted the arrangement, but I explained good-naturedly, "I think Ernest Tubb done it this-a-way. And like E. T., there'll be hell to pay if I find anybody in my seat. Just ask Little Lulu!"

I could have driven instead of assigning the extra deputy, but I wanted to use the road time for planning sessions. I sent Marvin to one of the bunks in the back to catch up on his sleep.

This hostage situation had given me renewed zeal for hostile action. I was backsliding on my new-found irenic state of mind. I began telling Meredith my scheme. "We'll call in helicopter gun ships. They'll come in just over the rim of the canyon, then drop down and shoot everybody in sight. There'll be complete surprise, and the enemy may not even get off a shot. On the second pass others may have been drawn outside in alarm. We'll pick them off. The buildings there are few and most of them not all that stout. If we don't get a white flag, we'll just cut everything apart on the third pass."

Meredith, of all people, made a gentle attempt to draw me back from rashness. "I see, Sheriff Bannerman, that you have made no allowance for negotiation."

"They've been negotiating all this time, that's why Tom Lenard called me. I'm known for decisive conclusions."

Meredith chuckled.

I took the light moment as a cue. "We've got to get on an informal basis. We're going to be working close together for a week or so. What do you say?"

"Suits me. I have a natural, some would say preternatural, preference for formal address. I confess that I resort to that style also as a means of fending off unwelcome familiarity in certain situations, such as dealing with an importunate client, back when I had clients, or facing a lawman who is investigating me on suspicion of murder! But you are right. Call me Alex. If you don't mind, I'll continue to call you Sheriff. Many of your co-workers do so, and the *nom de gendarme* has a curious combination of familiarity and respect, like 'Skipper' for the commanding officer of a naval ship or squadron."

"That's fine, podnuh. Tell me, what is an 'importunate' client?"

"I'll give you an example. John, a high school classmate of mine, years later had amassed a fortune in the meat-packing industry. I was rich myself by then. He liked to contract with me although my fee was more than he needed to pay for the fairly elementary projects he undertook. I think his impulse stemmed from a lingering envy of my status *vis-à-vis* his in our high school years. It is my conjecture that he took satisfaction in 'hiring' me, just as he would hire one of his hog slaughterers.

"On one of his projects, nothing more than a warehouse, albeit a gargantuan warehouse, I had to seek some artistic satisfaction in the work, and so lowered an infinitesimal portion of the ceiling to accomodate a stylistic flourish on the exterior.

"John accompanied me on a tour of the facility when the construction was well underway. He had to crouch to enter a portion of the storage area, really only a small portion in the scheme of things, didn't make a damn bit of difference, had to crouch under the five-foot ceiling, and emerged saying to me, 'Alex, you'll have to raise that ceiling.'

"I made no reply. That's when he became importunate. He demanded. When that didn't work, he cajoled. He repeated, 'Alex, you'll have to raise that ceiling.' 'No, John, I won't. You'll have to remember never to send anybody but short people in there!'"

I bent double laughing, an unaccustomed posture for me.

"The nerve of him," Alex said, "thinking that mere wealth could give him supremacy over an architect!

"Now, Sheriff, about the plan. I have no compunctions about mowing them down, to use the underworld argot, but there may be unforeseen problems, including the presence of wives and children and perhaps hostages. At least let us consider a contingency plan. Something is hatching in my mind, a consideration of entry through the tunnel. But I'll want to reconnoître on site before trying to spell it out."

I drew out the few newspaper clippings on the stand-off that Fanny had been able to gather from the *San Antonio Express-News,* the *Austin American-Statesman,* the *Houston Chronicle,* the *Fort Worth Star-Telegram, The Dallas Morning News,* and the San Angelo *Standard-Times.* Much was duplicative, being Associated Press copy, but some of the papers had sent their own writers and photographers to Fillmore County. Pack journalism made some of their copy virtually the same, too. Fanny had consolidated the grist to simplify the read. With it were a few faxes that Sheriff Lenard had sent following his call to me.

Alex, Pepys, and I went through it, learned what we could, and realized we could reach no conclusion on the plan until we got to Coal Mine Ranch and did our own investigation. O. B. was offered the clips and faxes, scanned them quickly, but gave his attention to radio reports he was getting through a headset. Equipped for the hopeful musical group, the bus had headsets at every seat. A selector would get you any one of nine stations the driver tuned on the receiver.

After listening to what little news there was from Fillmore County, O. B. switched to a western swing station. Being on a band bus again made him feel he had left something behind. He didn't have his bass fiddle with him. Or even a steel.

Marvin was still out of it, getting much-needed winks in the bunk he occupied.

West on Interstate Ten we went. We had boarded so quickly in the early morning dark we were oblivious to what was drawing gawks and stares and finger-pointing from passing motorists. Because of what was emblazoned in gaudy design and color on the band bus, our fearless law force was on its way to save the citizens of Fillmore County with the billing "The Doo-Dad Desperadoes."

Chapter Sixteen

BEN and O. B. sat together on the bus. They enjoyed the camaraderie of chummy antagonists who spoke bluntly to each other, all in good cheer.

"I'm surprised you agreed to help flush out the militia," Ben told O. B. "Rebelling against the government would be just fine with you. That's what I thought."

"That's why your liberal newspaper gets everything wrong, Ben. You don't care about the facts. You and Molly Ivins. I don't know why you run her left-wing stuff."

"It's not a liberal paper. You take the view that anybody who believes that Supreme Court decisions are the law of the land is a liberal. I run Molly's column because I know one reader who takes so much pleasure in it. That's you, O. B. You read every word, fuming, snorting, cursing. In other words, doing what for you is the acme of real fun."

"Do you know Molly Ivins?"

"I met her one time. I met her and Larry McMurtry on the same occasion. I wish you had been there."

Larry McMurtry sat there on the front porch of Judge Roy Bean's saloon in the town of Langtry, Texas. The judge sat there, too, but he had fallen asleep, passed out.

Larry was not the tracker Billy Williams had been in his prime, but Larry's eyesight was keen. About two miles distant he spied a puff of dust kicked up by a horse's hoof.

He could tell the rider was tall, probably a six-footer. It couldn't be big Hergardt. Even at that distance Larry could tell the rider looked intelligent, savvy, and witty. As Larry had said, "Hergardt was so dumb he often put his boots on the wrong feet. Later, he would wonder why his feet hurt." Hergardt was so dumb he looked dumb at a great distance.

Minutes later the horse was being reined in, just feet from the porch.

As the tall rider dismounted, Larry cried out.

"Molly Ivins!"

"Howdy, Larry."

"Molly, we haven't seen each other for some twenty years."

"Let me tell you something, good old boy. I'm looking for Ledge. Expect to find him just across the border from Presidio."

"Molly, I thought you and old Ledge always met in Austin."

"You're right, we used to, but I've heard he's staying at Ojinaga. I know I've always been hard on him, even mean to him. But now I know I love old Ledge. I've got to find him."

"It's happening to all of us old timers," Larry replied. "There are not many of us left. It's hard to figure, but we crave the old days so much we'd settle for meeting up with our old enemies one more time. I'd even like to see old Pox Pox."

"I remember last year when he burned Geebush," Molly said. "That was ugly. Pox Pox just likes to burn people."

"He burned Bubba pretty bad, too," Larry said. "He'll travel great distances to find somebody to burn. Famous Shoes was by here last week, said he'd seen Pox Pox's tracks. He could tell by the tracks that Pox Pox was on his way to the District of Columbia to burn the Vice President."

Larry saw another puff of dust, about a mile away this time because his eyesight wasn't as good as it used to be.

Larry looked at the rider. He was a short fellow. One of his big ears was pointed wrong. It went out of his head at an angle. Larry first thought it might be Ross Perot, but then knew it was Pox Pox.

When the short fellow drew up to the saloon and dismounted, Molly saw burnt flesh from head to toe, not to mention from ear to ear.

"Yup," Pox Pox said, before they could put the question to him. "The Vice President got the drop on me, so to speak. Torched me pretty bad. My burning days are over, that's my guess."

Their preoccupation with Pox Pox kept Larry and Molly from seeing the puff of dust a little less than a mile away.

When the rider and his mount neared the porch, Molly declared, "That's a stranger. We don't ever run into strangers out here, Larry, just folks we haven't seen for some twenty years."

Larry then spoke to the stranger. "You're a stranger. What are you doing out here?"

"I'm a writer. I've come out here to write about Texas."

Larry and Molly choked down an impulse to get Pox Pox to burn him. They didn't like the idea of anybody else starting to write about Texas.

Larry had learnt a lot from Billy Williams and Famous Shoes. He didn't miss a thing. Spying some gilt lettering on the fellow's saddlebags, Larry said, "You're Benjamin Edes."

"How did you know my name? That's like something that would happen in your book, *Streets of Laredo*. Your novels, and especially this one, are strong on realism, yet they're surrealistic. They also match Pearl Buck's sensitive depictions of people living just on the edge of survival. You're some talented writer."

Larry was glad he hadn't provoked Pox Pox to set fire to the stranger.

"You liberals are all alike," O. B. said to Ben. "You either take things too seriously, which is most of the time, or you make jokes out of things that matter. To get back to your question, you should know I'm not sympathetic with these militias. I don't join anything. No hate groups, no love groups either."

"Cable told me you were about to join the Sons of Confederate Veterans, but with the membership application they sent a flyer declaring they were not an extremist organization. So you wouldn't join."

"Damn right. I don't belong to anything but the V.F.W."

"What's wrong with the American Legion?"

"V.F.W. has a better bar. Back to the militia. Another reason I'm going to help Cable wipe 'em out is that if anybody takes over this country, it's going to be me."

"That's a lie. You wouldn't give up your independence even to be *in charge* of some organization. I'll tell you what I believe, O. B. In spite of your raving, I'm convinced that down deep you still really love the good ol' U. S. of A."

O. B., maybe to avoid comment, maybe in dismay, let out a deep, prolonged sigh.

Swinging the bus into the Fillmore County Courthouse parking lot, the driver pulled to a stop with the hiss of air brakes next to the spot where Tom Lenard stood. Our force had arrived in Collamer, the county seat. Sheriff Lenard boarded and the bus pulled away as he said howdies all around.

He gave directions to the driver and then told me, "I've got a spot all rigged for you—power, water, septic exchange, phone lines, the whole works. You'll be in sight of the tunnel entrance. In case you're not impressed yet, listen to this: I'll have you closer than the TV worry warts!"

When my crew and I were established in the command post, which the bus had become, I saw the now-idle Fillmore County deputies pointing at the bus and laughing. One of them walked up to me and asked, "Are you the head Doo-Dad?" Lenard was grinning as for the first time I had a good look at the gaudy bus.

"Get some tarps thrown over it. I don't mind you guys ribbing us, but I'll be damned if those TV airheads are going to get a shot of it."

Sheriff Lenard provided several copies of a list of the militia members. "Just fifteen?" I asked.

"Really just nine. Look at the last six. Women. Camp followers, we believe."

O. B. spoke up. "At last we've got a militia that behaves like real men. Maybe I'm on the wrong side in this war, too."

I said, "It's a relief to know there are no wives and children in there. It uncomplicates the operation. Plus we won't have innocents on our conscience. But we sure are contemplating a big and costly attack, just to go after nine mavericks."

Lenard smiled. "Remember the Union force that was attempting to dislodge a Confederate position on a hillside manned by one Rebel? A platoon leader sent ten Yankees up there. Nine were shot by the fedary and one came back to tell how tough it was. A captain stepped in and said, 'Send a larger force.' Thirty went up and one came back. 'What the hell's the trouble?' asked the general. 'Why can't you get one Rebel? Send a bigger force.' When sixty Yankees failed, the one who returned faced a blistering tirade from the general. 'But sir,' the Yankee private protested, 'we're outnumbered. There's not just *one*, there's *two* Rebels up there!'"

O. B. said, "That anecdote brings to mind Lee's first words to Grant in the Appomattox Court House."

"His first words?" Lenard asked.

"'What say we make it best two out of three?'"

I gave one of the copies of the list to Pepys Fowler and spoke with her briefly. She got in one of the patrol cars provided by Fillmore County and took off.

"I'm going back to Collamer," Lenard said. "It's all yours out here now. Call me if you need me."

Alex had his surveying instruments set up and was taking sightings on the tunnel entrance.

I put Fanny Wright in control of the

communications gear in the bus, now including a computer and modem.

Marvin, wider awake than anybody else now, was getting acquainted with the deputies and guardsmen assigned to duty under my command.

"We're starting this thing without an operations order, O. B." I said. "How in hell can we work without an op order?"

"We'll just write one," O. B. replied. "Great thing is, we won't have to get anybody's approval on it."

The two of us went back on board the bus and I added to Fanny's duties. "We're writing an op order. O. B. will do the thinking, you'll put it all in your computer and print it out, and I'll sign it." Fanny and O. B. knew that in the actual division of labor, I would shoulder my share of the load.

Pepys had used the car phone to scare up a little information on the militia men whose names were on the list. On the third go she hit something she thought was promising, and turned the car toward Van Horn. When she got there, she took a motel room. Early the next morning she would be *tête-à-tête* with Mrs. Craig F. Ely. Janet Ely in no time would be looking on Pepys as her dearest confidant. When Pepys left, Janet left with her.

Pepys had recognized one name on the list. She drove now toward Saragosa to make the confirmation. Finding a little tea room just off the main drag, she pulled in. Having Janet in tow made the situation even chattier. From a couple of the ladies having brunch, Pepys learned what she needed to know. Conjecture confirmed. The identification was made. She and Janet began the drive back to Coal Mine Ranch.

It was time for the "general staff" to put the pieces in place. Marvin, Pepys, Fanny, Ben, O. B., Alex, and I sat around a pull-down table in the band bus. Janet Ely was reading a magazine in a mobile home that had been moved in nearby.

Pepys, who never waited to be asked, spoke up first. "Cable, before you lay down your grand plan, you've got to know one thing I found out. What do you know about Linda Faye's first husband?"

The truth was, very little. Linda Faye had reverted to her maiden name after the divorce, and I couldn't even call the ex's name to mind.

"I saw his name on the list, Felix Post, and over in Saragosa determined that it is indeed he. Linda Faye's ex is there yonder in Coal Mine Ranch, armed and dangerous."

"And in danger himself," I added. Linda Faye had no lingering affection for Felix Post, far from it. Nothing but hostility had been left for a long time. Still, Pepys' disclosure added a complication to the decision on the mode of attack. Would I be willing to give orders that would result in the killing of Linda Faye's ex?

No one else spoke, but there were troubled minds all around the table as Fanny handed out copies of the op order. They read in silence until Ben spoke. "You three have put together a model of brevity. Had I known op orders could be like this, I might have stayed in the service."

"Everything needed is in there," O. B. said. "We left out all the boiler plate that armed forces people put in there just to cover their asses."

"We don't need to cover our asses," I added, "just

because they are *our* asses. And because this damn thing is going to work!"

"Likely it would work," Alex said, "but let us consider an alternative. These sketches," he continued as he displayed them on an easel, "show that a fairly large area directly in front of the mouth of the tunnel is safe from any trajectory from possible weapons on the peaks. Thus we are provided a working area in which to assemble our menagerie."

Menagerie? we all thought. *What is he talking about?*

"I have surveyed the rails and find they remain sound. Of course I cannot be certain of the last twenty feet or so, out of sight beyond a slight curve. If the rails turn out to be disrupted there, the problem is not insuperable.

"With Fanny's help, I've been in touch with the West Texas Wildlife Preserve in the Sierra Diablo Mountains. They have been re-stocking the puma. They have about a hundred in the preserve right now, slated for release back into the wild.

"They will cooperate with us. They transport them here, we load them in their cages on trams, and with an engine trailing, drive them to the other end. There, radio controlled locks are opened, and the puma roar into the militia compound. The vandals, terrified, run for the hills, in a manner of speaking. Your troopers easily pick them off, preferably by capture."

No one at the table was more stunned than I. It was daring, it was ingenious, hell it was bizarre! But would it work?

Ben was all for it. Anything that would reduce, maybe eliminate killing.

Pepys conceded the scheme could silence

opponents of harsh governmental action, but warned that the SPCA would be down on our heads.

O. B. lamented the need to re-write a perfectly beautiful op order.

Marvin had a suggestion. "We could make this Plan A. What's already been written could remain in as the contingency plan."

Consensus ensued. We could sleep on it, then continue working the complex logistics that either plan would entail. Or both plans. That was another suggestion made as we were getting up from the table. "Loose the pumas on 'em," O. B. said, "then blow hell out of 'em from the gunships as they run in disarray."

"Ben, I want you to come out and meet Janet Ely," Pepys said. "This is for public relations, so all that the rest of you need to know is that Janet is the wife of one of the militia members, but she wants the law enforced. She's mad as hell that her husband is in there making it with one of their whores!"

After talking with the vengeful wife, Ben returned to the bus and took a seat by Alex. "Tell me, how do you square your enthusiasm for public housing with the extreme individualism that's implied by your evident fondness for some of the writings of Ayn Rand?"

"I am no libertarian! I recognize the seeming contradiction, but we, all of us, are bundles of contradiction. Things are never as simple as lawmen, editors, or some academics think they are."

"I believe I see the common thread," Ben replied. "Either position takes arrogance. Arrogance on the one hand that you may kill with impunity. Arrogance on the other hand that your solution—public housing or whatever—is the right solution and must be forced on the masses by the power of government."

Alex beamed. Ben's explanation fit him, but he was not going to acknowledge it in words. Instead he took another tack. "Ah, youth! ... when you only halfway know things, but fully believe things. The young intern, Fanny, thought she really had something when she came across the little play. Ha! She had it wrong. The arrogant character of the play is dead, or presumed to be, before the drama begins. He never appears. He did not commit murder. In principle, however, she did understand the thrust of the play."

"I will concede this much," Ben said. "It would have been an injustice to hold you responsible for each and every book found in your library. Visiting the Little White House in Georgia when I was a youngster, I looked at the volumes on the shelves next to the chair in which FDR was sitting when he was stricken. His thoughts might be understood, it occurred to me, by knowing the books he had around him. I soon realized, of course, that you never know why a book is there, or whether the owner has even read it. I have books in my library that people have given to me. I can't stand to throw books away, any books. I hope I'll never be held responsible for a certain book in my library, which I've never read, a particularly trashy little book of fiction that reposes there."

When the bus was calm, I called Linda Faye. She was fine, little Matt was fine. Then I told her that her ex, Felix Post, was one of the renegades in the box canyon. Linda Faye was not surprised. "I haven't kept up with his movements for years, but it's the kind of thing he would do. He was always angry at the whole world, thought he was always right and everybody else was wrong. Especially me. I was always wrong."

"Linda Faye, this may be the last thing he does. Depending on how we decide to attack, and how it turns out, he may lose his life."

"There was a time, when I was still married to him, I would liked to have seen you charge in like a knight in shining armor and get him out of my life. No I wouldn't. I never liked that way of settling things. But you know what I mean. Now, I hope you don't kill him. I don't care what happens to Felix Post, but I care about you. Just because I used to have a connection with him, you might always have it on your conscience. Cable, try to work it out where nobody gets killed."

"You know I trust your instincts. I'll try."

After a little loving chit-chat, we hung up, and went to bed hundreds of miles apart.

Chapter Seventeen

ALL the next day was spent gathering and collating intelligence and firming up assets.

One of my old Army buddies was now c.o. of a national guard unit in the Panhandle. He had agreed to send the gunships. No state call-up was necessary; they would make the attack on their regular drill weekend. The c.o. had informed the adjutant general and the governor through a double blind. They were all for it but wanted deniability. It would just be a unit operation. I got on the line with the c.o. and reconfirmed the arrangements, also asking for a photo recon immediately.

Alex got the aerial photos, including some stereo pairs, by day's end. In the meantime he had made other assessments of the target and got reassurance the pumas would arrive as scheduled.

O. B. and Fanny stayed in the command post relaying radio, telephone, fax, and e-mail traffic and compiling new data in the computer file. Much to

Fanny's annoyance, O. B. kept saying, "This militia thing is a real rat-fuck."

Pepys and Ben took Janet around to the TV crews, who just about peed in their pants over the choice breaking news that was being handed right to them. What the pair was up to was engendering public support for whatever action the task force eventually took. TV news bought it hook, line, and sinker.

At dusk they met around the table again. Pepys was elated at the reception they had gotten from the TV crews and from the print and radio journalists as well.

"If we play our cards right," Pepys told them, "we'll have N.O.W. in here carrying placards in favor of us and against the militia. They're sympathetic to the wives, of course, and they also oppose the degradation of the women who are being used as prostitutes."

"You mean," O. B. asked, "they're opposed to the fact that six women are *not* being screwed, and also opposed to the fact that six other women *are* being screwed?"

"Hush up, O. B. It's because of men like you that we need N.O.W."

Now down to grim business.

Alex reported surveillance that showed the mavericks were well-stocked with provisions. Besides, they were in possession of about fifty head of cattle and had started a vegetable garden. The women were tending the tomatoes, corn, onions, and okra. There were three wells on the ranch, powered by windmills. They would be able to make a long stand of it unless killed or driven out.

"Alex," I said, "one thing your puma plan is lacking is containment. That's a good-sized area in there. Suppose our targets just scatter when they see the cats?"

"The point is conceded. I have been reflecting, too, on the mistake often made, of using yesterday's solutions for today's problems. Rather than getting *in* to the target, as I did at the Swinton residence, we want to deter the targets from getting *out*. If you go with the gunship plan, the targets take cover in the tunnel. But they won't run to a tunnel from which hungry pumas are emerging.

"Remember the words of Charles Dickens: 'Ride on! Rough-shod if need be, smooth-shod if that will do, but ride on!'"

I was elated. "I believe we've talked ourselves into a solution!" I set it out for them in detail, and then Fanny and O. B. wrote it into the op order. Saturday would be the day. Just as the rising sun could first be seen in the West Texas sky would be the time.

All the assets were in readiness.

I was aloft in one of the gunships.

Alex stood by the technicians who would control the puma train.

O. B. had declared he would never get in a plane again after his last B-29 raid on Tokyo in 1945. He had kept his vow. He was in the command post with Fanny.

Pepys and Ben made a strategic feint, going over to the press compound with more angry wives in tow. Pepys and Ben would miss all the action. They were seeing to it that the newsies would miss it, too.

Marvin was coordinating the ground troops from a tent within sight of the tunnel entrance, on higher ground.

First the pumas. Exactly on the minute planned, the train began slowly moving into the tunnel. Exactly on the minute planned, the cage door sprang open on the first tram to emerge into the box canyon. Then another, and another. One hundred pumas were loping this way and that, some of them making straight for the stone structure being used as the militia's fort. One lookout stood duty during the dog shift. The shift was near its end, and for a change the lookout was wakeful. First he detected only movement. He rang the great ranch bell. Then in disbelief he made out the lunging shapes of pumas. He turned and headed for the fort.

His eight confederates, some still pulling on their trousers, ran toward him, rifles at the ready, grabbed him and turned him around, and headed for the pumas. But which way was toward the cats? There were pumas to the left of them, pumas to the right of them. The renegades were in this state of disarray when they first detected the sound of the choppers. That wasn't a bad idea the lookout had had, they suddenly realized. They turned and ran for the fort.

One of the camp followers, more nearly wide awake than the other five, had stirred at the first peal of the alarm bell. As soon as the last of the militia men had run from the building, she had sprung from bed, caught sight of two or three pumas, and bolted the heavy door. Then she woke the other women. The shutters were already closed and locked. They watched through peep holes as their erstwhile protectors and masters scrambled first toward the pumas and then away from them. They stayed at their peep holes as the masters pounded on the great door seeking entry.

What to do?

The gunships were hovering. The pumas were prowling. Influenced by Linda Faye and Ben, I had gotten another helicopter added to the fleet, a personnel carrier. It took center stage now. The pilot, using his p.a., offered the mavericks a free ride.

"Put down your guns. We'll descend, and transport you."

There was no movement by the renegades. The pilot noted the prowling pumas and realized the nine feared for their lives and thus were reluctant to shed their rifles. The genius of the American fighting man is the capacity for independent decision making. The pilot made one.

"Okay, keep your guns. Show me a white flag."

There was hurried consultation on the ground. One of the members took off his khaki shirt, then removed his white t-shirt and hung it on a tree, all the while clumsily trying to keep his eye and his rifle on the nearest pumas.

Down the chopper settled. One by one the militia men headed for the hatch. Each would drop his rifle when close to soon-to-be-airborne safety from the fierce cats. The camp followers, watching the proceedings through their peep holes, then unbolted the door and did what camp followers do. They followed. Two guards who had deplaned provided cover for them. With fifteen passengers on board, guarded by armed troopers, the chopper lifted away.

They were to head to the helipad at the county jail, but my command chopper had to descend to let me off, so by prearrangement the troop ship landed as well, near the band bus. *Look out for your troops* was my motto, and for morale I wanted my crew to see vivid evidence of their success: the captured militia and their camp followers.

The landing also provided me my first glimpse at Felix Post. I got one of the guards to call the prisoner's name. Post acknowledged with a halfway raise of his left hand. He didn't look like much to me, surly and a little paunchy. Partly I was curious; partly I wanted to be able to give Linda Faye a report of my own personal confirmation that Post had not met a violent end at the hands of my troops.

I radioed Sheriff Lenard to report mission accomplished. Then I called Linda Faye. Ben transmitted a brief fax to the press compound which sent them scurrying to the county jail in hopes of getting something on the new prisoners. Pepys responded to the message by turning loose her entourage of militia wives, all of whom also headed to the jail. Pepys returned to the command post area.

Her return set off a second round of back-slapping all around as I repeated my "well dones."

"Strike the tarps," I cried. "Let's get this thing back to Gilgal."

Utilities had been disconnected. All hands boarded and the bus pulled away, soon out of sight of the tunnel to Coal Mine Ranch.

Heading back to I-10 on the one street that went through Collamer, the bus slowed at the intersection at the courthouse and jail area for a blinking caution light. That's when a CBS twinkie spotted the now uncovered gaudy paint job on the bus. A frisson of adolescent delight, of the kind that only television newspeople can feel, went through the twinkie. "An actuality!" "An EXCLUSIVE!"

Patched in live to CBS's newscast, shots of the moving bus were transmitted as the voice-over warbled, "And now they depart, mission accomplished, the aptly named Doo-Dad Desperadoes."

EPILOGUE

I waited until we had gone about twenty miles, allowing the bus to cross the Fillmore County line. I was still deputized there. Officially I was on leave from the office of sheriff of Joshua County and in any case was off duty. I signaled Marvin, who then headed for the sole locked cabinet. Taking a tiny key from his vest pocket, and straightening his badge, he opened the cabinet door.

"Drinks are on the house!" I declared. All hands ordered bloody Marys; O. B. specified gin as the active ingredient in his.

There was no shortage of subjects for toasts. The first was to Tom Lenard, who had set us in motion. Hurrahs went up for the real Doo-Dad Desperadoes, the little band in Junction. O. B. toasted N.O.W.

No house limit was set. Some had a second round; others had more. Having gotten to know each other pretty well by working together several days, we now got better acquainted still.

When we reached the town of Fort Stockton, the driver took the US 285 exit and pulled in at a service station to gas up. Although we still had ample provisions on board, all of us welcomed the chance to get out and stretch our legs and to make selections from the snack stand.

Upon alighting, we were surprised by a welcoming committee of some twenty or thirty citizens. A few held hastily lettered placards. News reports of the decisive rout of the militia had made folk heroes out of my crew. Two-way radio communication between Tom Lenard and the driver and Lenard and the Pecos County sheriff had made possible the reception for the heroes at the service station.

Back on I-10, sated with gin and vodka and notoriety, my crew were a happy crew. O. B. declared that he had enjoyed the whole expedition so much, but particularly being back on a band bus, that he was going to put together a western swing group, get Stroud to play harmonica, and go back on the road.

"You're too old for that," Marvin said.

"You can't be too old for it, just too young for it. I was too young when I used to do it. So young I damn near got myself killed."

When we had traveled seventy-two miles from Fort Stockton, the driver, again on cue from Tom Lenard, pulled into a convenience store at Sheffield. The celebration was not a surprise this time, but it was fun all over again.

Ozona and Sonora did not rate stops, and Roosevelt got just a wave. We especially looked forward to Junction. It was next to our home county and enthusiasm figured to be high. This time it was I who alerted my counterpart in Kimble County.

Nobody was disappointed. We stopped at the Coke Stevenson Center. Having plenty of time to prepare, the folks carrying placards were more numerous than at the earlier stops.

Late in the day we finally drove the last short leg from Junction to Gilgal. We found the whole court house square covered with people. Nothing like it had been seen since political rallies of pre-TV days.

Linda Faye and Matt just got quick but intense hugs from me before I took a p.a. microphone to thank the folks for coming out and for their support during the Coal Mine Ranch operation.

The Gilgal High School band, being led for a year by Robin F. A. Fabel, a visiting director from Britain who had introduced the members to some unfamiliar charts, began playing "In a Monastery Garden."

Deputies in patrol cars stood by to provide rides to crew members who needed them. Linda Faye had brought Matt in the "cable car," and I got in with them. At home, we let Matt stay up until he became sleepy.

Then Linda Faye and I sat together and talked.

"Your advice was good, Linda Faye, as usual. You saved me from doing something I shouldn't have done, and besides that, it might have all blown up in my face if I had tried it."

"Things don't happen overnight, Cable. Things that are real important to us don't. You've got to give Ben credit for helping you do things to understand this, over a couple of years' time."

"Well, I do. You know, I even give credit to Felix Post, as odd as that may sound. When I looked at him, I thought to myself that he was not even worth killing."

"You can say that again! But I know what you mean. That's good, Cable, you see it like that now."

"See, even on the way out there, I was thinking about doing things my same old way."

"You mean you went out there looking forward to killing the members of the militia?"

"That was on my mind. When I learned there were six camp followers in there, I didn't want to hurt them. It'd be a shame to kill six willing women!"

"Shame on you, Cable!"

"I think it's a good sign that I can show some humor on the subject."

"It is. But you're naughty."

"Who my daddy was doesn't torture me anymore."

"I'll tell you, there's something a lot worse than knowing who your daddy was and regretting it."

"What's that?"

"Knowing you're the parent of a bad kid, and wishing you weren't. That's something you can't hide from. It hurts every day, when you dread hearing the phone ring and it being another call from the police. And worse, dreading to see your kid show up, to torment you all over again, maybe even do you harm."

"You sound like you speak from experience."

"No, thank God, I haven't had that experience, but a real close friend of mine did, and I sorta suffered through it with her. That's how I know how bad it can be."

"Speaking of kids, being a father has had as good an effect on me as anything, and I owe that to you, too."

We were both getting sleepy, and Matt would be hungry for some breakfast in a few hours. Off to bed we went.

The next day was a full one for me. Besides

catching up on accumulated paper work, I had a number of thank-yous to send around by telephone and fax.

One key call was incoming. In Fillmore County there was no woman deputy, never had been one. Tom Lenard called, asking me for help again.

"I've just had a deputy quit. I know it's trans-Pecos Texas, but we can't go on forever without a woman on the force. What little I learned about that little intern's work on the operation impressed me, and I know she doesn't have a job yet. Can you recommend her?"

"Absolutely. She's tops. I'd hire her myself, except there's no opening. I'll get her on the phone."

Fanny, who had stayed over a day to help Pepys with the backlog, took the call. Lenard made the offer and she accepted.

I could hear the squeal from down the hall. I stepped into the corridor where I saw Fanny heading for me, followed by Pepys. "I haven't heard a squeal like that since sorority pledge day, and you're just one woman."

"My job starts one week from today! It's not the place of my dreams, it's not Dallas, but Collamer here I come!"

Pepys hugged her and congratulated her.

"I appreciate it, Sheriff Bannerman," Fanny said. "You have got me my first job in law enforcement. Well, my first real job. I mean, well, it was real being here, but, I mean, I'm not an intern anymore!"

In the time they had been gone, the D.A. had made no move on a re-trial of Meredith. I got Alex on the phone to thank him again for his work on the Coal Mine Ranch operation.

Although Gideon Lincecum had delighted in

making the unusual defense that Meredith had insisted upon, he had used excruciating care to avoid the introduction of palpable evidence before the jury. His stratagem was to let the murder remain, as much as possible, a figurative rather than literal event in their minds. At his insistence, Meredith answered "I do not remember" to each question concerning firing the weapon, disposing of the weapon, even going to the Swinton residence. Because he had willingly taken the stand, he could not invoke Fifth Amendment privilege against possible self-incrimination. The prosecutor pushed hard, and the judge repeatedly directed Meredith to answer, but if you don't remember, you don't remember.

The ploy succeeded. At trial's end, nothing was known of the weapon and little was known of any of Meredith's actions in the crime. I had remained curious. Now, with a re-trial unlikely, maybe Alex would confide in me. The architect's vanity had made him loathe to follow Lincecum's instructions during the trial. He was inordinately proud of his excellent memory, indeed, his power of total recall. My simple request was all it took to set Alex talking.

"Once a mystery is exposed, there is nothing mysterious about it. The disrobing, as it were, is akin to seeing stage scenery from behind. The thrill is gone.

"I did not simply assume that Swinton would recognize the threat implied in the now notorious letter to the editor that I penned. I had conversed with him, from time to time, as I attempted to persuade him to abandon his niggardly attitude toward public housing. We had discussed Richard Daley and his blunt order, 'Shoot to kill.'

"Likewise, we had discussed Walter Gropius.

Swinton, I learned, was fairly well-read, and he was already familiar with Gropius when I brought up the name. Yes, he knew who sent him the skeleton key, and he knew who had visited his little lavatory and left him dying.

"The weapon? Ha! So much is made of tracing a weapon, and disposing of a weapon. Well in advance of the execution, I went to Fort Worth to a gun show. Those affairs are virtually uncontrolled, but in any event, who can keep up with little transactions at an independent dealer's table, or for that matter, from his truck in the parking lot? As it happened, I bought the gun at a table, in full view, had they cared to watch, of hundreds of people. Right after firing the weapon into the Swinton residence, I drove to San Antonio. My timing had nothing to do with the day of your re-election, Sheriff. There was a gun show in progress. I sold the gun at a small profit!

"I have put the whole Swinton matter out of my mind. I am going to do some hours of community service although I have not been sentenced to any."

"Public housing?"

"Exactly. It is time I put an oar in, rather than grousing from the shore."

The visit I wanted to make, felt like I had to make, would have to wait until tomorrow.

Ben said yes, he could take half the day off from the paper. I drove over to *Harry's of the West* to pick him up.

"Where are we going?" Ben asked. He had stopped and was standing by the open passenger door.

"There's a cave I want you to see."

"Damned if that's so! Fool me once, that's your

fault; fool me twice, that's my fault. You're not going to get me in that cave and draw a gun on me again."

"C'mon, Ben, you know I'm past that."

"Just kidding." Ben got in the patrol car.

At the ranch, I again took the Jeep, for Ben's sake. As we drove across the ranch, I explained that Texas law on cemeteries was astoundingly loose. You could declare your ranch, your lot if that's all you had, or any little part of it a cemetery. You just made your declaration to the county clerk, no restrictions, no questions asked.

"Doesn't astound me," Ben said. "Texas has been such a wild place, still is, that you need to be able to bury 'em right where they fall. It would put a sheriff, or even a private citizen, to a hell of a lot of trouble to be carting corpses around, of the people he killed, to get 'em buried."

"I can do without your sarcasm. Anyway, first thing this morning I registered with the clerk. Declared the cave a cemetery. That way, I don't have to call attention to the events of long ago. Word has gotten around, I know. But scuttlebutt is one thing, moving all those skeletons is something else. We'd have to have hearings, bring everything out. I don't want to expose my granddaddy's crime—if it was a crime. Another reason is to let them keep resting where they've rested for so long."

There had always been a breeze when I had come to the cave before. Today it was still. A bright sun blistered the place.

"I've been back out here since that day you and I came out of the cave," I said. "That's the part I like to remember, not us being inside but coming out of the cave. The stone count matches the body count, give or take one or two."

Ben saw that I had piled the stones back. Just as before, they concealed the mouth of the cave. Right now they did not look as one, but they would weather again as they had in the years following the villainy.

"The count could be a coincidence, but I like to think of it another way."

Ben knew what I meant.

"There's been enough killing. Too much killing. Then, and lately. Me, I'm done with it. For that, I owe you a lot, Ben. I still put a lot of stock in the actual experience, but I believe I see now what the 'higher learning' you like to talk about is for. It gives you the framework to make sense out of what happens.

"Ben, I've got to ask you to do one more thing for me."

Ben was deep in thought, happy for me, his protégé. Now he stirred. "What's that, Cable?"

"Help me with this rock. It wasn't in the pile before. I want to put this one up there for my natural daddy."

Ben was glad to have something to do, not to have to have anything to say.

Together we hefted the last rock into place.

"You said one time there wasn't one, Ben. But you can regard it this way: It was done by unlikely hands. But we're looking at it, Ben.

"There is in Joshua County a reminder of stones."

Cable's Acknowledgements

I get the last word. That's an unaccustomed privilege for me. Ben usually gets the last word.

Although even Stroud doesn't understand Stroud, as Ben has said, I understand enough to have had some idea how to tell this story. I give a big Texas "thanks, podnuh!" to Oxford Stroud.

Ward Allen would not have interested himself in these proceedings, you might think, but he did. Professor Allen is author of *Translating for King James* and co-author of *The Coming of the King James Gospels*. I must absolve him of any responsibility for Ben's meandering exegisis, but Ward did point me to the equal opportunity passage in the Book of Joshua. The great Bible scholar preferred to give his attention to the kinds of automobiles that Lucky Garrison sold at the Equal Opportunity Car Lot. I am in his debt.

D. Harkey, ranching consultant to the stars, counseled me on stocking the Bannerman Ranch, pasture management, and all sorts of things. The cows he told me to put there, I put there. Harkey and I agreed that if your column ran in more than one newspaper you're a syndicated columnist. He's a syndicated columnist. Like me, he's an Aggie who thinks and writes, which is not so exceptional as some Tea Sippers would have you believe. D. Harkey is a fellow I really appreciate.

Ray and Mary La Fontaine, co-authors of *Oswald Talked*, are Texans I think a lot of. They read *A Reminder of Stones*, made invaluable suggestions, and were enthusiastic *compadres*.

The Saga of Packer the Cannibal to which I adverted in my re-election campaign speech came from a book by Richard Erdoes, *Tales from the American Frontier* (New York, Pantheon Books, © 1991, Richard Erdoes, $25.00). Thanks for permission to use the excerpt.

I appreciate Citizen Caine letting me use the satire on privies. It first ran in the *Mountain Sun*, Kerrville, Texas, in 1993.

Thanks to Leland Smith and *The American Legion Magazine* for bringing Graustark to mind. This fictional country in Europe was the setting for the 1926 Marion Davies film *Beverly of Graustark*. Locating my combat experience there was a way to dodge the freight of the war I really fought in.

This is my story. The author named on the title page set it down on paper. He let me tell it my way. I appreciate it.

—*Cable Bannerman*